Summer in the Bayou

Miss Fortune World (A Miss Prim & Proper Mystery), Volume 1

Caroline Mickelson

Published by J&R Fan Fiction, 2018.

This is a work of fiction. Similarities to real people, places, or events are entirely coincidental.

SUMMER IN THE BAYOU

First edition. August 16, 2018.

Copyright © 2018 Caroline Mickelson.

ISBN: 979-8201919382

Written by Caroline Mickelson.

Chapter One

"NEXT STOP, SINFUL." The bus driver's voice rang through the crowded bus. "Anyone crazy enough to want to get off here?"

A wave of laughter rippled through the bus. Clearly the joke was something only my fellow passengers would understand. Seeing as I was from Boston, and had never been further south than Philadelphia, the humor was lost on me.

Encouraged by the response to his little joke, the bus driver looked up into his rear-view mirror and grinned. "Because I'm not crazy enough to stop here if I don't have to."

I stood up, remembering at the last minute to duck so I didn't hit my head on the overhead luggage racks. "Please stop, sir," I called out, somehow managing to be heard despite two days worth of thirst and dust lodged in my throat. "Sinful is my final destination."

A howl of laughter escaped an elderly man with a wizened face. "I hope it's not, for your sake." He grinned, exposing a mouth that lacked more than a few teeth. "You're too pretty a little filly to be facing your last stop in life."

I forced myself to smile, despite not finding his comments the least bit humorous. The man had to be sixty to seventy years my senior at the very least. Decorum dictated that I respect the elderly. But Sinful, a place I'd never visited, couldn't possibly be a worse place to spend my time than this bus had been for the past few days.

I'd just reached up into the overhead bin for my red vintage Samsonite suitcase when the driver slammed on the brakes. The bus came to a shuddering halt and I pitched forward, landing rather inelegantly in the lap of a gentleman who resembled a seedy Santa Claus.

With a startled cry, I jumped to my feet and apologized profusely while he got my suitcase down for me.

I'm Stephanie St. James, known to gentle readers of a Boston newspaper as "Miss Prim and Proper". I prided myself on my strict adherence to proper etiquette at all times.

With as much as élan as I could muster under the circumstances, I shuffled toward the front of the bus, my suitcase thumping each seat as I passed it. Despite offering a "pardon me" and an "excuse me, please" as I moved forward, I was given nothing but the stink-eye from my fellow passengers.

I stopped beside the driver's seat. "Thank you, sir, for ensuring our safe delivery to—"

He reached past me and jerked the lever that opened the door. "Lady, you want to thank me? Get off my bus."

Stunned, I lifted my chin, grabbed hold of my suitcase, and alighted. Once I had my two feet planted squarely on the ground, I turned back for one last look at the driver. Never one to end any conversation in a contentious manner, I bid him a good day. In answer, he drew the bus door shut and peeled away, leaving me standing in a whirling dervish of dust and dirt.

I held a white lace trimmed handkerchief over my mouth as the dust settled, grateful that I was where I needed to be at long last. I didn't know much about the town I'd just arrived in, but I knew that compared to that filthy bus, Sinful was going to feel like heaven.

I HEARD MY GREAT-AUNT Ida Belle's voice before I saw her.

"Lord above, I think that preppy little gal is my niece."

Two elderly ladies and a much younger blonde materialized in front of me. "Aunt Ida Belle?" I was only ninety percent sure that the taller of the two older women was my aunt. Truth told, I'd never met her in person. But, boy oh boy, had I heard stories. Most of them so wild I knew they couldn't possibly be true.

"Stephanie?" she said, confirming that my guess about which one she was had been correct. "Child, you're covered in dirt."

I picked up my suitcase and headed toward the gawking trio. I could only imagine how disheveled I looked. I held out my hand to my aunt. "It's lovely to finally meet you, Aunt Ida Belle."

Her eyes wide, she reached out and gripped my hand. "Welcome to Sinful."

"Thank you. I appreciate you and your friends meeting my bus." I waited for her to introduce me to her companions, but when she stayed silent I turned my attention to the other woman. This senior was much shorter than my aunt, although as far as wrinkles went, the two appeared to be in a virtual tie for who had the most. I smiled brightly. "Hello, I'm Stephanie St. James."

A wide grin stretched across her face. "I reckon we're in for a good 'ole time." She elbowed my aunt in the ribs. "Your niece looks like a cross between Mary Poppins and Jackie O."

I looked down at my shirtwaist dress, knowing that it boasted almost as many wrinkles as the ladies in front of me did. I reached up and smoothed my hair back. "I certainly would like to freshen up."

The younger woman held out her hand. "I'm Fortune. You'll have to pardon Gertie here. Not too many new people our age pass through Sinful." She cast a sideways glance at Gertie, who was still staring. "Let me take your bag and we'll head back to my house so you can get cleaned up. It's closer than Gertie's or your aunt's."

I smiled my gratitude and gratefully handed her my suitcase. Despite her lack of a Louisiana accent, her gracious manner was certainly southern. "Thank you. Your hospitality is much appreciated."

My aunt shook her head. "Well, my word, you're sure grown up, aren't you? I haven't seen your father since he was about five years old. How old is he now?"

I tried to hide my surprise. "Daddy passed on about a year and a half ago."

Embarrassment flitted over Ida Belle's face. "Sorry. I didn't know."

I followed the ladies through the parking lot until we stopped in front of a Cadillac that had not only seen better days, it had probably seen better decades. My eyes traveled over the length of it. I'd wager my last five dollars that rubber bands held it together. I watched in shock as Fortune slung my suitcase in the trunk. Was that pavement I could see through the bottom of the trunk?

"Don't worry." Fortune smiled knowingly. "The hole is too small for your luggage to fall through." She held open the rear passenger door. "Hop in and, whatever you do, hold on."

I got into the backseat at the same time Gertie slid in the driver's seat, but I'd barely shut the door before the engine roared to life and the Cadillac peeled away from the curb, its tires squealing loud enough to wake three generations of the dead.

"Hold on like I told you," Fortune shouted over the sound of the muffler.

I grabbed onto the side door handle just in time. Gertie peeled around the corner as if she were driving a stunt car in an old seventies movie. To avoid screaming out in sheer terror, I bit the inside of my cheek until I tasted blood.

"I heard you're in some kind of trouble, Stephanie," Gertie shouted. She caught my gaze in the rear-view mirror. "Ida Bella said—"

"Ida Belle says to keep your eyes on the road, you old fool," my aunt shouted. She shot an apologetic glance over her shoulder at me.

I did my best to muster a reassuring smile, no easy task when traveling at ninety miles an hour down a dirt road with Louisiana size mosquitoes making a beeline for my face through the open window.

Yes, I was in trouble. Deep trouble. And if I managed to live through Gertie's driving, I'd tell Aunt Ida Belle and her friends all about it.

After all, I'd come to Sinful to hide. And I was going to need their help.

Chapter Two

"SO WHEN'S THE BLESSED event?"

I took a dainty sip from the mason jar of sweet tea in front of me. All three women stared at me with wide eyes that reflected sheer terror. Fortune clung to the edge of the kitchen table, her knuckles white.

In my entire twenty-four years of life, I've never had trouble keeping up with a conversation, until this one. These ladies were a whole world unto themselves, and I was still reeling from Gertie's wild car ride to Fortune's house. After I'd showered and changed into a clean black linen skirt and powder blue cashmere sweater set, and once my pearls were clasped around my neck, I'd settled down for what I'd hoped was going to be a proper tea party. But it appeared that the word "proper" wasn't one I was going to be often using to refer to these three ladies. "I'm not sure," I hedged.

"We don't know nothin' about birthin' no babies," Gertie said.

"And we don't particularly want to find out either," Fortune said. She shot me an apologetic glance. "No offense or anything."

I looked to my aunt for an explanation, but she appeared to still be stuck somewhere between horrified and petrified. "Aunt Ida Belle? What are they talking about?"

It took her three attempts before her words were coherent enough to understand. "The growing problem you've been carrying around."

"Oh, I see. Unfortunately, it isn't going away, you're right."

"Cousin Mabel said you've got a little trouble on your hands. Is that right?"

I blushed. "Well, yes, but I'm not so sure it's going to stay little for long."

My aunt emitted a sound somewhere between a low moan and a groan just before her eyes rolled back in her head.

"She's going to faint," Fortune cried. "Gertie, do something."

I watched in horror as Gertie grabbed a pitcher of iced tea and hurled its contents straight into Ida Belle's face.

"What the hell did you do that for, you fool?" Aunt Ida Belle shook her head like a wet dog, sending a spray of sticky sweet tea everywhere.

A wave of foreboding crashed over me. I'd come to Sinful to hide with my elderly maiden aunt, but suddenly I realized that things here weren't going to turn out the way I'd imagined. Yes, Aunt Ida Belle was elderly, and an old maid to boot, but she wasn't at all what I'd expected. Right now she looked more like a prickly cactus than a shrinking violet.

We sat in a painfully awkward silence for several minutes as Ida Belle mopped her face with a wet towel while Fortune wiped down the kitchen table. Once order was restored, my aunt turned her attention to me. "Now, listen, young lady. While we're all women here, none of us has traveled the road that you're about to head down," she said, her voice stern.

"Well, that's a relief. I wouldn't wish this mess on anyone." I took another sip of my tea, grateful that it hadn't spilled in the earlier melee. I wouldn't say no to a cucumber sandwich, but none had been offered. Frankly, I'd expected a bit more from southern hospitality but, then again, an ideal guest shouldn't expect refreshments. I turned my attention back to the conversation at hand. "It all happened so quickly. When I first met Nikolai he seemed like such a gentleman. I never expected to end up in this situation."

"Ha!" Gertie slammed her hands on the table, causing us all to jump. "Isn't that the way men are? Tale as old as time." She shook her head so violently I was afraid it was going to fall off and roll across the room.

"Hush," Aunt Ida Belle chided. "Let the child tell her story."

Fortune leaned forward and looked at me, her gaze every bit as solemn as my great-aunt's. "So Nikolai is the man who's responsible for the trouble you're in?"

I shrugged. "I think so. But it might easily be Ivan, Vladimir, or even Mikhail."

"Stop!" Aunt Ida Belle pushed her chair away from the table and got to her feet. "I can't listen to any more of this."

"Sit down." Fortune pointed to the recently vacated seat. "We can't run from this. And you know as well as I do that we need all the facts so we can handle whatever's going to happen."

Aunt Ida Belle sank into her chair. "You're right. Go ahead, Stephanie. How many more men are out there who could be involved in this?"

"Well, it's hard to be precise. But I think Sergei might be the only other one that could have been involved."

"You think?" Gertie gave a low whistle. "You don't know for sure?"

Again, I shrugged. "I can't be quite certain, I'm sorry. It all happened so quickly and I was enjoying myself so much that I didn't quite calculate the risks as carefully as I should have. I see that now. But it's too late to change anything."

"So you've considered *all* your options?" Fortune asked, putting an especially heavy emphasis on the word "all".

"Yes, and it seemed to me that the best way to handle the situation was to leave town and hide somewhere where no one knows me. Does that make sense?"

All three women nodded.

"So, cousin Mabel suggested that I look you up, Aunt Ida Belle."

"I just bet she did, the old cow." She scowled. "But you're here now. We'll help you. Won't we, girls?"

Gertie and Fortune nodded in unison. But neither spoke. Frankly, they looked shell-shocked.

Not that I blamed them. The conversation was bewildering. "Thank you. I'll do my best not to be a burden."

We sat in silence for several more minutes. The only sound in the room was my growling stomach.

"So when's the baby due?" Gertie asked.

"What baby?" I frowned.

She nodded sagely. "I've heard of that. I think they call it pregnancy brain."

"What?" And then slowly all of the strange fragments of conversation began to slot into place. "Wait, you think I'm pregnant?"

"Aren't you?" Aunt Ida Belle asked.

"No, of course not. Good heavens, Aunt Ida Belle, where would you get such a far- fetched notion?"

"Well, Mabel said you were in trouble. In my day, when a girl was 'in trouble' it only meant one thing."

"That she was knocked up," Gertie added. "So you're not? Knocked up, I mean?"

"No!" And even if I were, I'd never use an expression as tacky as that to describe my delicate condition. I shuddered.

"So exactly what sort of trouble are you in?" Fortune asked. "And who are those men who you were just listing?"

"They're, well, I'm not sure how to delicately put this—"

"We don't have time for delicate," Fortune interrupted me. "Give it to us straight up. We can't help you out if we don't know what kind of trouble you're in."

I opened my mouth to explain but my words were cut off by the sound of shattering glass and a spray of bullets whizzing overhead.

Chapter Three

"GET DOWN," FORTUNE yelled.

At least, I think it was Fortune. It was hard to make out whose voice it was over the sound of my own high-pitched screams. Aunt Ida Belle grabbed my arm and shoved me under the table. When I opened my mouth to scream again, she clamped her hand over the lower half of my face.

"Hush, child," she hissed. But it wasn't her whispered warning that silenced me. It was the sight of a gun in her free hand. My eyes widened until it felt like they were going to pop right out. Frantically, I looked at Fortune and Gertie to judge their reaction to the fact that my aunt was brandishing a weapon like some sort of common criminal.

But I quickly saw that if they cared at all, they'd be impressed. Her gun was almost twice the size of the ones they were holding.

I strained against her hold on me.

"I'll let you go, Stephanie," she whispered in my ear, "but if you so much as blink twice, you're going to be sorry. Got it?"

I nodded, careful to only blink once. I didn't know this woman well but the intensity in her eyes and the vise-like grip she had on my wrist told me she was serious.

"Gertie, call the police." Fortune glanced first at Aunt Ida Belle and then at me. "You both okay here?"

"We're fine. Just be careful," Aunt Ida Belle said.

Fortune nodded and crept out from under the table. By now the volley of bullets had let up, but who knew for how long? I opened my mouth to ask where on earth Fortune thought she was going, but one glance at my aunt made me think better of it. I could wait to find out.

I watched Fortune crawl along the floor toward the staircase as I heard Gertie murmuring into the phone. Nothing made any sense. Why was Fortune going upstairs? And why weren't Gertie and my aunt having an attack of the vapors right about now? If this wasn't an appropriate time for one, I couldn't imagine when would be.

The sound of shattering glass stopped, but that might have been because all of the kitchen windows had already been blown out. I wasn't about to stick my head out and count. Instead, I held my breath. Was this a cease-fire or was someone reloading? But the silence stretched on for several minutes until finally all we heard was the sound of our labored breathing.

"Looks like they've cleared off," Gertie said. "I'm heading out."

"Right behind you," Aunt Ida Belle said. She gave me a gentle shove and I crawled out from under the table, although I'd have preferred to stay right where I was.

"Mind the glass. We've got more important things to do than play triage tonight." Gertie held out a hand to help me up, which I gratefully accepted. My knees were shaking as badly as my hands, we're talking Richter scale trembling. I'd have gladly plopped down on a kitchen chair, but they were all covered in shards of glass.

"Shouldn't one of us tell Fortune she can come out of hiding now?" I asked.

For some odd reason, this seemed to amuse Gertie. She let out a howl of laughter. "Fortune doesn't hide from anyone, girl. Oh, wait, maybe that's not technically true if we count—"

"Be quiet, Gertie," Aunt Ida Belle snapped. "Fortune isn't hiding, Stephanie. She went upstairs where she's got some kick ass powerful binoculars so she could try to find out who the trigger happy moron is."

Right on cue, Fortune jogged down the stairs and into the kitchen. Her eyes scanned the room first before she turned to look at us. "You all okay?"

Gertie nodded, Ida Belle grunted, but I couldn't do more than stare dumbly. I felt like Dorothy must have when she landed in Oz. Fortune, however, appeared to be on top of her game.

"Look, we'd better get our stories straight before Carter gets here. There's no way he's going to believe that we were trying to chase off a raccoon." She rolled her eyes. "And I keep thinking that things can't get any more awkward between us."

"Who's Carter?" I asked.

"Forget the coon story," my aunt said, ignoring my question. "Once he gets a ballistics report, he's going to see that we were on the receiving end of some serious firepower."

"Which means..." Gertie stopped speaking when Fortune and Aunt Ida Belle nodded their agreement to whatever it was she'd left unsaid.

"Which means what?" I said, looking between them. "What aren't you telling me?"

Finally, I had their attention. All three women turned to look at me.

"I think the real question," Fortune asked, "is what aren't you telling us?"

The last thing I wanted to do was admit what kind of trouble I'd brought to their sleepy bayou town.

The squeal of tires outside and the slamming of a vehicle door granted me a reprieve. Within seconds, someone was pounding on the front door.

"That's Carter," Fortune said, her eyes focused on me. "He's the law here in Sinful."

"Okay," I nodded my understanding. "So I tell him my story?"

"No," all three women shouted in unison.

"Stephanie St. James, you listen to me, child," my Aunt Ida Belle said, one hand clasped on my arm. She gave me a gentle shake. "You know nothing. You say nothing. Not until after Carter's gone, got it?"

"But—"

"But nothing," Gertie hissed as Fortune headed for the front door. "Not a single word. Lives depend on it, and not just yours, you hear?"

I nodded, but not because I truly understood. I was beyond confused. Fortune, a girl pretty enough to be a beauty queen, had fire in her eyes. Gertie and Aunt Ida Belle had morphed from two wrinkled old ladies into CIA agent intense mode.

It suddenly made sense why I was the only one who got off the bus in Sinful. The people in this town were just plain crazy.

"Don't even mention the word raccoon." A surprisingly young, not to mention handsome, sheriff's deputy held up his hands as he entered the kitchen. "If you can't tell me the God's truth about what happened here, then y'all just stay silent, you hear?"

Silent we stayed. I looked at Aunt Ida Belle, who looked at Gertie, who looked at Fortune, who looked at the ceiling. They seemed united in their silence, but I couldn't remain quiet.

Good manners dictated an introduction, irrespective of the fact that someone had just tried to annihilate the four of us. I firmly believe that once our society loses our civility, we lose everything.

I felt the glass crunch underfoot as I stepped forward and held out my hand. "It's a pleasure to meet you, sir. Allow me to introduce myself." No one else was about to do it for me, it appeared. "I'm Stephanie St. James from Boston."

"Deputy Carter LeBlanc." His handshake was firm, his demeanor professional, but something in his gaze when he looked at the four of us was downright weary. "I'd like to welcome you to Sinful but it looks like someone else beat me to it." His appraising gaze swept through the kitchen before returning to rest on me. "I have a load of questions for all of you, but first, tell me how you know these ladies."

"Certainly, Officer LeBlanc." I smiled my most congenial smile. "It just so happens that Miss Ida Belle here is my great-aunt on my father's side of the family."

His eyebrows shot up. "You're related?"

"Yes, sir," I said, more than a bit of pride in my voice.

But Carter didn't look impressed. He looked downright horrified. "So now there's four of you?" He wiped a hand across his brow. "Damn."

Chapter Four

"DEPUTY LEBLANC CERTAINLY seemed out of sorts, the way he stormed out of here muttering under his breath," I said not long after Sinful's deputy sheriff had departed. After he'd helped us nail boards up over the shot-out windows, and before he'd departed, he warned us upside down and backwards not to leave the house until morning. Carter's demeanor vacillated between threatening and begging. "Is he always like that?"

"Like what?" Aunt Ida Belle asked. She pointed to my broom. "Keep sweeping while you talk. You can do both at once, can't you?"

I resumed shepherding broken glass into piles with my broom. "He seemed exasperated. Well, no, that's not the right word. I can't quite put my finger on it—"

"Only Fortune's allowed to put her finger on Carter," Gertie said with a wicked grin. "Ain't that right, Fortune?"

We all looked at Fortune, but she didn't respond. She sat lost in thought, the only one of us not working to restore order to her war zone of a kitchen. Aunt Ida Belle let out an ear-splitting whistle.

Fortune jumped to her feet. "What?" She looked from one of us to the other. "What's wrong?"

"You tell us." Ida Belle's frown was fierce. "Your mind's a million miles away and yet we've got trouble lurking right around us. Not a good combination."

Fortune neatly sidestepped my piles of glass as she took a mug out of the cupboard and filled it with the coffee that Gertie had just made. "I was trying to remember exactly where I've heard that unique pattern of gun fire before." Her brow furrowed, she took a long, slow sip. "The bullet release pattern is not standard for an American-made semi-automatic."

I stopped sweeping and stared at her. "You heard all that over the sound of breaking glass and my screams?"

Her eyes narrowed, but only for a moment, as if she'd drawn a curtain over them and I wasn't supposed to see what was behind her thoughts. "I took a military history course in college," she said. "Weaponry happens to be a little something I studied one semester."

I looked away and resumed sweeping without saying anything. If I had nothing left in this world, I still had my manners, which dictated that I not call my hostess out as a liar in her own home. But Fortune was lying. I, too, had studied military history in college, and none of those classes had taught us a darn thing about how to differentiate between the varying sounds of modern artillery.

"What are you thinking?" Aunt Ida Belle pulled up a chair and sat, her eyes fixed on Fortune's face. "Out with it. You've got something on your mind."

Instead of answering, Fortune shot me a quick glance.

"Oh, go ahead," my aunt told her. "Stephanie's plum stuck in the middle of this like the rest of us are, she won't be any trouble. I'll see to that."

I continued sweeping, heeding my aunt's words. I knew little about this woman, but I'd decided that she was formidable. I was going to stay on her good side while I was here in Sinful.

"Those were Nikonov assault rifles if I'm not mistaken. Unless they were Kalashnikovs. Either way, they were Russian made."

I froze. "Did you say Russian?"

All eyes turned to stare at me.

"Russian, huh?" Gertie said. "Would this have anything to do with the list of names you were rattling off earlier? Let's see, there was Vladimir—"

Rude as it was, I cut her off right there. "I had very few interactions with Vladimir." After all, I had my reputation to protect, and being associated with Vladimir, however indirectly, wasn't going to help it. But a quick glance at the boarded up windows reminded me that I had something else I should be worrying about protecting. Namely, my life. "There's probably a little something I should tell you all."

"Go on, Stephanie," Aunt Ida Belle encouraged me. "Whatever it is, we can handle it."

This I very much doubted. I told them as much. "Please understand that I don't mean any offense," I hastened to add. "But you and Gertie are well into your golden years, Aunt Ida Belle. I'm up against something serious here."

Aunt Ida Belle slammed her hand on the table. "Enough of this beating around the bush, missy. Who's after you?"

I hesitated. I'd come to Sinful to hide, not embroil my great-aunt and her friends in a dangerous situation. But the hiding obviously wasn't working. The people looking for me clearly knew where I was. Their welcome volley of bullets had sent that message loud and clear. I could run, but they weren't going to let me hide.

Crestfallen, I plopped down in a chair. "Maybe I should leave in the morning."

Fortune shook her head. "They'll follow you wherever you go. You're safer here."

"But if I stay, I'll be putting you three in danger." I turned to my great-aunt. "I'm sorry, Aunt Ida Belle, I really didn't think they'd find me so quickly."

She patted my hand awkwardly. "You're just going to have to trust us with the truth. Now, I'm asking you for the last time, who's after you?"

"The mob." I half-expected them to not believe me. After all, how many elderly southern women had any experience with organized crime?

"The Russian mob?" Gertie's eyes about bugged out of her head. "You're kidding me."

I sighed. "I wish I were. But I'm not."

"Who exactly are we talking about?" Fortune demanded. "Which family?"

"Sidorov."

Fortune gave a low whistle. "How deep are you in?"

I swept my arm around the kitchen. "Deep enough that they followed me all the way down to the backwaters of the bayou." I buried my face in my hands. "I don't know what to do now."

"I do."

I lifted my head and stared into my Aunt Ida Belle's eyes. "You do?"

"Sure I do," she said. "It's obvious, isn't it, girls?"

Gertie and Fortune both nodded.

"What am I missing?" If I didn't know any better, I would swear that the three women I sat with looked almost animated by the direction our conversation was taking. I, however, was hovering somewhere between shocked and horrified. "What are you proposing we do?"

Fortune smiled. "We're going to get them before they get you."

Chapter Five

OUR GAME PLAN, COBBLED together over a late night meal of turkey sandwiches and chocolate chip cookies, made sense before we'd all headed to bed. However, in the light of day, as the sun was blocked from streaming in the kitchen windows by the boards we'd hastily nailed up the night before, I was suddenly much less sure it made any sense at all.

The four of us against the Sidorov family? The idea was sheer folly.

But Aunt Ida Belle shot down my concerns every time I tried to give voice to them. Her refusal to even hear me out put me in a tenuous position. Even though we were Fortune's houseguests, Aunt Ida Belle was still technically my hostess, not to mention that she was far older than I was, and a relative to boot. How could I argue with her?

"Now stop trying to squabble with me," she chided me as I washed up the coffee mugs. "We're not going to sit around in this house like four scared ninnies. We're going to go about our day as planned. End of discussion."

I sighed. "What are our plans for the day?"

She nodded approvingly. "That's a girl. Just do as we say and everything's going to be fine."

Fortune bounded into the kitchen wearing a bright yellow cotton t-shirt, black yoga pants, and shocking neon green tennis shoes. I gave her appearance a once-over as she did the same to mine. At the other end of the fashion spectrum, I'd chosen a light shell pink cotton blouse, a white cardigan, a knee-length black A-line skirt and black ballet slippers. I hardly need add that I also wore my pearls. After all, this was summer in the south. Pearls were a must.

Gertie grabbed her two-ton purse off the counter and slung it over her shoulder. "Doesn't hanging out with these two young things make you feel about twenty-five again, Ida Belle?"

"I'll answer that tonight if none of us ends up with a bullet lodged in our brain." She looked at Fortune. "Buddy McBride's coming by to replace your windows?"

Fortune nodded. "He's coming at ten, so let's clear out of here. My mouth's watering just thinking about one of Francine's breakfasts."

We piled into Gertie's Cadillac and began the wild ride toward the center of Sinful. As her ancient rust-mobile lurched to a stop in front of Francine's Diner, I realized I'd now cheated death three times in twenty-four hours. Between Gertie's driving and the Russian mob, if I survived my summer in the bayou, the Pope should classify it as a miracle.

Francine's was exactly what I expected an old-fashioned, small time southern diner to look like. If it had been updated any time within the past twenty years, someone had taken great pains to hide the fact. But once we tucked into the heaping plates of fluffy waffles, tender scrambled eggs, and savory sausage links, I understood Aunt Ida Belle's insistence that we come here for breakfast. While I hoped this wouldn't be my last meal on this earth, if it were, at least I'd had a sneak peek of what food in heaven must taste like.

"Now let's talk turkey." Aunt Ida Belle pushed away her empty plate. She fixed her eyes on me with that laser intense stare of hers. "What have you got that the Ruskis want?"

"Did you steal something from them?" Gertie's eyes sparkled with excitement.

"Not exactly," I hedged. Despite the fact that I was related by blood to one of the women I sat with, I still wasn't overly comfortable sharing such personal details. Especially considering that sharing said details might well end up getting them killed.

"You know, Stephanie, you're in a no-win situation here." Fortune's expression was sympathetic. "And I know you don't know the three of us from a hole in the ground, but you've been marked."

My eyes widened to hear my situation put so bluntly into words.

"Ignoring this isn't going to make it go away," Fortune pressed on. "We need the details and we need them now so we can keep you safe."

My expression must have conveyed my skepticism because Aunt Ida Belle jumped into the conversation, her expression stern and her tone authoritative.

"Stephanie, I didn't go looking for any trouble, but courtesy of that old fool Mable, you've brought it straight to my doorstep. You and I are kin, and that still holds meaning with me. I'll protect you, but I won't put up with any half-truths or partial stories about what's going on. Is that clear?"

I nodded. She was pulling rank. She knew it and I knew it. And honestly, what other options did I have?

"Good." Satisfied her point was made, she settled back in the booth, a half smile on her face. "You don't need to understand how we work, you hear? Your job is to answer any question we ask, truthfully and immediately."

"Yes, Aunt Ida Belle."

"Now, start at the beginning and hurry up to the end so we don't have to walk around Sinful with invisible targets on our backs."

The beginning? I guess that would be my job. "Back home, I write for the *Boston Daily News*. I have a weekly column on the finer points of etiquette, and I have a daily segment that answers readers' questions about how to handle awkward social situations."

"So you're like Miss Manners?" Gertie asked.

"Actually, I'm Miss Prim and Proper." I wasn't the least bit surprised when Gertie let out a whoop of laughter that had heads turning in our direction. Neither was I surprised by Fortune's barely concealed smirk. Aunt Ida Belle's expression was unreadable. "Thanks in large part to the internet, newspaper circulation is way down. While I'm still employed, I've had to take on a side job or two to make ends meet."

Gertie's eyebrows shot up. "You became a mob escort?"

"No, of course not." I took a slow sip of my coffee so I could have a moment to compose myself. One day in Sinful wasn't going to turn me into a harpy who snapped at senior citizens, even if they were accusing me of upscale street walking. "I placed an advertisement in the paper offering my services as a protocol consultant."

"And how much work did that bring in?" Fortune asked.

My false pride urged me to exaggerate, but I was mindful of my great-aunt's earlier warning to be honest. "About as much as you'd expect."

She nodded. "Not much."

"Precisely. So when I received a telephone call from one of Mr. Sidorov's personal assistants, I was delighted." There was no need to tell them about the stack of unpaid utility bills that had prompted my happy dance when I heard the sum of money I was being offered.

"They offered you a wad and a half, didn't they?" Gertie asked. "These mob types are always waving around fistfuls of cash like flags on the Fourth of July."

I resisted the urge to ask Gertie just what personal experience she'd had with the Russian mob. There was nothing to be gained by embarrassing her when she had to admit she had none. "Let's just say they offered me enough so that I could keep my prize Persian in cat food for the next decade."

"And what specifically were they wanting in return for the generous pay?" Aunt Ida Belle asked.

"Initially, I advised the members of Mr. Sidorov's personal staff on the finer points of fitting into Boston society." Such as, one did not order shots of vodka with orange juice at corporate breakfast meetings. Nor was it considered top shelf to wear a purple suit to a funeral. "Trust me, it was basic manners tutoring, nothing more."

"Well, something had to happen or they wouldn't have followed you all the way down here and shot up Fortune's house, huh?"

"Point taken, Aunt Ida Belle." I quickly filled them in on all the little tasks I undertook for the family. "But it was all innocent enough. They wanted to be considered classy like the Kennedys, but no matter how many times I tried to tell them that the Kennedys weren't the standard bearer of class, they wouldn't listen. They're a stubborn lot who don't like to hear the word "no"."

"Funny thing about members of organized crime," Fortune said. "They like to give orders, not take them."

"I figured that out, trust me."

"So what made you run?" my great-aunt asked.

"Mikhail. The Sidorov's youngest son. Everyone calls him Misha. Let's just say he developed a bit of an unhealthy attachment to me."

"Ha! A man was in the middle of this." Gertie pumped her fist in the air. "I should've taken bets this morning. I knew it."

The rest of the story just tumbled out. I'd increasingly become uncomfortable not only with the people the Sidorovs surrounded themselves with but also with Misha's attentions. "He insisted that we were engaged, a lie his father believed." I could feel my face flame as I remembered how persistent of a suitor Misha had become. "He even told his father that he'd executed a man in front of me and now we had to get married so I couldn't testify against him."

Gertie shook her head. "The boy sure doesn't know much about how to woo a woman, does he?"

"Did he execute someone in front of you?" Fortune asked.

"No, good heavens, no." I shuddered. "But I wouldn't put it past him. Which is why I found a cat sitter and got out of town. I never want to see Misha Sidorov again."

Fortune's cell phone rang and we waited in silence while she took the call. Her face barely registered any emotion as she listened to the caller, but her words sent a chill right through me.

"Don't touch the body, we'll be right there."

Chapter Six

ODDLY ENOUGH, AS WE raced out of Francine's, just barely slowing down long enough to throw two twenty-dollar bills in the direction of the cash register, no one seemed overly surprised at the sight of four grown women tearing out of the diner as if the gates of hell were about to close behind us.

"Get in," Gertie yelled as we neared her rusted-out Caddy.

She needn't have worried. Fortune all but shoved me in the back seat before she dove in on top of me. Aunt Ida Belle swung into the front passenger seat as if she'd been riding shotgun with Gertie for decades, which she probably had. Gertie peeled out onto the main street and gunned the car back toward Fortune's house.

Luckily no small children were playing ball in the street. Otherwise, Gertie would have added to Sinful's growing body count.

"Hurry up," Aunt Ida Belle egged her on. "We've got to get there before Carter does."

"Why?" I asked, but no one answered my question. I didn't even bother with the other two questions I was desperate to have answered. Whose body was it and where was it? I'd see in due course. Assuming I survived the car ride.

"What else did Buddy McBride say?" Aunt Ida Belle asked, glancing over her shoulder at Fortune. "He recognized the body?"

"I didn't ask."

Despite the warmth of the mid-morning sun, I shivered. I'd run away from the Russian mob to find a quiet place to hide, but in less than twenty-four hours we'd been shot at and now there was a body we were rushing to get a look at before the police did. Why weren't my companions panicking? If anything, they seemed energized by the race towards the corpse. For the first time, I wondered if I'd have been safer hiding out in Boston.

"Let's hope that fool takes his time calling the sheriff's department." Gertie swung wide around a corner as we neared Fortune's house. "I was his English teacher for three years running. Let's just say, that boy was a little short in the initiative department."

Because Buddy's truck was parked in the middle of the driveway, Gertie guided her Caddy straight up and onto the lawn. I gasped at her lack of decorum. Parking on the street in front of a home was one thing, but on the lawn? Mercy.

My companions didn't try to contain their delight that no law enforcement vehicles were in sight.

"We beat 'em," Gertie called out triumphantly over her shoulder as she bounded toward the house.

"Let's just hope it's not Buddy's glutton of a brother-in-law who had a heart attack in Fortune's kitchen," Aunt Ida Belle chimed in as she hurried to catch up with Gertie.

But it wasn't Buddy's brother-in-law we found dead on the kitchen floor.

It was Misha Sidorov.

A wave of nausea rolled over me as I stared down at Misha's lifeless body. I clapped my hands over my mouth to keep from screaming.

I'd never seen a dead body before, nor do I ever want to again. Misha's baby blue eyes stared straight up at me. I couldn't help but feel that their empty gaze was almost accusatory. My knees buckled and I reached out for something to hold on to.

"Gertie, grab a chair." Fortune slipped her arm around my waist and I willingly sagged against her. "Ida Belle, why don't you take Buddy outside and see what he can tell you?"

As I sank into the chair Gertie brought over, I glanced up at Buddy. He looked about how I felt. Shocked. Numb. Horrified. But I doubt he felt even a drop of the guilt that was threatening to engulf me. I covered my face with my hands and groaned.

"Stephanie, listen to me." Fortune knelt beside me. "Who is this man? You recognize him, don't you?"

I nodded. "It's Misha. No, I mean, it was Misha. Oh, I feel sick."

"Stephanie, pull yourself together. The police will be here soon, so first you need to tell me what you can." She stepped in front of me to block my view of Misha's body, but not before I saw Gertie kneel down beside him.

"What's she doing?" I demanded.

"Praying?"

I peered around her to get a better look at Gertie. "With her hand in Misha's pocket?"

"She's looking for his ID," Fortune assured me, sounding more confident this time.

"I just told you who it is," I said. I wasn't going to wrangle with the past tense. So long as his body was in the same room as me, I was using present tense. Propriety and grammar be damned.

Gertie sat back on her heels. "I can't find any ID on him. His wallet is stuffed with cash, but there's no driver's license." She blew out an exasperated breath. "Not so much as a library card."

"Really, Gertie?" Fortune's words were laced with sarcasm. "Hard to believe that any self-respecting mobster would go out without laminated incrimination in his wallet. Focus, woman. Carter's going to be here any moment. What else is he carrying?"

"He's packing a nice piece." She pulled out a Makarov pistol and held it up. "I wouldn't mind keeping this one for myself."

"Oh, he loved that gun." I felt tears prick at the back of my eyes. "He never went anywhere without it."

"Well, he can't take it with him so there's no sense in letting it go to waste." Gertie shoved it in her purse.

"Put that back," Fortune demanded. "We don't have time to bail you out for petty theft and obstruction. If you want a gun like that then you save your social security checks and buy one on the black market like everyone else."

Gertie slid Misha's gun back into his holster. "Fine. Spoil my fun."

"Fun? Did she say fun?" I could hear the hysteria in my voice. I looked up at Fortune. "This isn't funny."

She patted my shoulder in an awkward attempt at reassurance. "I know. We're just trying to gather information so we can find out who did this to Misha. And to find out who's gunning for you."

I shivered. I'm not going to pretend that I was devastated that Misha was dead. I wasn't ever in love with him. And I was more than a little frightened by how obsessed with me he had been. But there was a bit of sadness mixed in with all the other emotions swirling around in my head.

I knew who was "gunning" for me, as Fortune put it. The Sidorovs. All of them would be out in full force once they heard that Misha was dead. I'd be to blame even if I wasn't the one who killed him.

"How did he die?" I asked. The question hadn't occurred to me before now. There wasn't blood splattered everywhere, well, anywhere in fact. Not that I could see. I stood and peered around Fortune. Misha lay still, as if he were asleep. Except that his eyes were wide open. That was seriously starting to freak me out.

"I don't know. I'll take a look." Fortune motioned for Gertie to come stand next to me. She knelt beside Misha and studied his still form. She didn't touch him, but she didn't shy away from examining him either.

Suddenly it occurred to me that the way Aunt Ida Belle, Fortune, and Gertie were acting wasn't the way that three women would normally act in the presence of a strange corpse. They appeared curious and galvanized for action. Where was the panic? The swooning? The vapors?

"Carter's coming," Aunt Ida Belle's voice rang out from the front door. "Haul your carcasses out here, ladies."

Fortune shot to her feet. She and Gertie each grabbed one of my arms and hustled me out to the front porch just as Deputy LeBlanc's pickup truck came tearing around the street corner.

Fortune leaned in close. "Pay attention, Stephanie. Answer all of Carter's questions honestly. But don't volunteer information. We need to keep our cards close to our vests if we are to have a chance of keeping you safe. Understand?"

I nodded. Not because I actually understood, but because the look on Carter's face as he got out of his truck was thunderous. I decided then that I'd be safer with the ladies. At least they were unlikely to haul me in on suspicion of murder.

I wasn't so sure I could say the same for Sinful's deputy sheriff.

Chapter Seven

BEFORE CARTER EVEN stepped one boot on the front porch step, Ida Belle, Gertie, and Fortune all broke into speech at once. Carter stuck two fingers in his mouth and emitted an ear-splitting whistle that was so loud, I was surprised it didn't wake poor Misha.

"Do. Not. Say. One. Word." Carter brushed past us and breezed into the house. "And don't move either," he called over his shoulder. "Y'all stay put until I come back out or Deputy Breaux arrives."

An eerie silence descended over the five of us. I took my first good look at the man who'd found Misha's body. Buddy McBride was likely in his mid-forties, no older. He wore a dingy used-to-be-white t-shirt with "Got Glass?" emblazoned across the front. He held a Georgia Bull Dogs baseball cap, which he was twisting near to pieces. I'd never seen the man before, but one thing was clear. He looked miserably uncomfortable. I felt for him.

"Am I in trouble, Miss Gertie?" Buddy asked in a low whisper, his eyes darting toward the house.

Gertie leaned past me to look him square in the eye. "Did you kill that man in there?"

He shook his head vehemently. "No, ma'am, I did not."

"Then stick with that story and you're fine." Gertie looked over her shoulder to see if Carter was coming, but the coast was clear. She turned back to Buddy. "Now, I remember that time when you were in the fourth grade and Lester Williams threw his baseball straight through the library window. You remember that, Buddy?"

35

He gulped. "Yes, ma'am, I do."

"Then you also remember when you swore up and down that you didn't see who threw the ball, but all along you knew it was Lester. You remember that, too?"

Buddy nodded earnestly.

"I covered for you with the principal because I didn't want you getting in trouble for being a loyal friend." Gertie paused for a moment to let Buddy catch up before she went in for the kill. "Now, I figure that means you owe me. Don't you, Buddy?"

Aunt Ida Belle, Fortune, and I exchanged glances. I sensed they were as impressed with Gertie as I was. The woman was smooth, I'd give her that.

"I reckon it does, Miss Gertie."

"Good boy. Now, you tell me what you saw in there. Mind that I only want the truth."

Buddy nodded, bit his lip, shifted from foot to foot, and would have continued squirming if Aunt Ida Belle hadn't elbowed him in the ribs.

"Well, it's like I told Miss Ida Belle, I didn't really see nothing."

"Anything," Gertie corrected him.

He nodded. "Right, anything. I didn't see anything. I was working alone because Lazy Davy called in sick this morning. He's been doing that a lot lately."

With a name like Lazy Davy, how could this surprise him?

"So, I'd finished chipping out the glass still stuck in the window frame," Buddy continued, "and then I headed out to my truck to get my vacuum."

"When did you first see the man in there?" Fortune asked, her voice low. "Did you see a car or hear anyone else?"

"I already told Miss Ida Belle everything," Buddy protested. He licked his lips and his hands shook. "It's all so confusing."

Gertie reached into her bag, rummaged around, and pulled out a small bottle. She handed it to him. "Take a sip and then get back to your story. Hurry now."

Her former student didn't hesitate. When he tipped back the bottle I saw the words "Cough Syrup" printed on the front of the bottle. Cough syrup? Buddy hadn't coughed once. But he gave a contented sigh after two long swigs.

I felt like I'd just disappeared down the rabbit hole. Everything was making less sense as time wore on, not more.

Aunt Ida Belle grabbed the bottle out of Buddy's hands and handed it to Gertie, who capped it and tossed it back in her shoulder bag.

"Did you see anyone at all? Or hear anyone?" Gertie demanded.

Buddy shook his head. "Nothing, I swear. I went out to my truck and was digging around the back for my vacuum. There weren't no cars going by and I didn't hear a thing. Course, I had my music up kinda loud." He reached into his pocket and pulled out an iPod shuffle and ear buds. "And I had my back to the street while I was looking for my extension cord."

So Buddy McBride was officially of no help. Perfect.

We were standing in frustrated silence when Carter came back out of Fortune's front door. He looked around, a frown on his face. "No sign of Deputy Breaux?"

Fortune shook her head. "None."

Carter swore under his breath. His obvious frustration notwithstanding, I hardly considered this appropriate behavior when ladies were present. I couldn't help myself. I had to say something. "Deputy LeBlanc, I'll remind you that there are ladies present."

His eyes widened. He looked at Fortune. "Is she for real?"

Fortune nodded wordlessly.

Carter turned to face me. "I mean no offense, but this isn't a ladies social. My job is to find out who killed that man in there."

"Who is he?" Gertie asked, her voice as innocent as an angel. "I mean, who was he?"

Carter crossed his beefy arms across his chest. "Don't tell me that you don't know."

"I don't know," Buddy said. "I've never seen him before in my life."

I was saved from having to lie, or confess, by the arrival of two cars. A man in uniform, presumably Deputy Breaux, got out of the first vehicle. A woman in a hideously loud floral print dress got out of the second. The deputy moved deferentially aside as the woman slammed her car door and strode toward the house.

"What on earth is going on here, LeBlanc?" she demanded.

"Is this the police commissioner?" I asked.

"Ha!" Gertie snorted derisively. "She couldn't even get elected as mayor without causing a fuss."

"Shut up, Gertie." The woman turned to look me up and down from my ballet flats to what I hoped was my still perfectly coiffed chignon. "Who is this?"

I don't mind admitting that I took an immediate dislike to the woman in front of me. Her scornful expression was enough to curdle fresh milk. But regardless of her poor manners, I still had a reputation to uphold. I held out my hand. "My name is Stephanie St. James. I'm Ida Belle's great-niece from Boston."

Her face contorted. "Another Yankee?" She shot a disdainful glance at Fortune. "That would explain you being smack in the center of trouble."

"What are you doing here, Celia?" Carter asked.

"I was at the police station looking for you, and Myrtle told me that you were here. I decided to ensure that you were here on official business and not on a social call."

I saw Fortune's hands clench into fists. Clearly, there was a tense history between these women. Whoever this Celia was, she was trouble. Trouble in an ugly dress.

But what about Misha? His body was just lying in there. Surely he should take precedence over the bad blood between Fortune and Celia? "Trust me, this is official business," I said, carefully choosing my words to not give away that I knew the victim. "If you don't believe us, go in and take a look. There's a dead man in there."

Celia drew herself up and squared her shoulders. "Maybe I will. As Sinful's mayor, I certainly have the right."

Carter waved the other deputy over. "Stay here with Buddy and the ladies. Don't let them talk." He waved for the mayor to precede him into the house. "Hurry up and view the body, Celia. I've got a crime scene to process."

She stomped past us into Fortune's house but was back out within the space of less than two minutes. She glared at us all. "I knew you were up to monkey business." She wagged her finger at Fortune. "I should have you brought up on charges for filing false police reports. And your boyfriend is going to lose his job if it's the last thing I do."

She stormed out to her car and peeled away from the curb just as Carter reappeared on the porch. He looked about ready to have a stroke.

"What the hell is going on here?" he demanded. "Where's the body?"

We all stared at him.

"What are you talking about, boy?" Ida Belle demanded.

"He's gone." Carter pointed toward the house. "The body's gone."

Deputy Breaux spoke for the first time. "Are you sure he was really dead?"

Carter let loose with a stream of cuss words that proved he must have been bayou-born and bred. They were words I'd certainly never heard before.

Without waiting for permission to move, Gertie and Ida Belle charged into the kitchen. Fortune and I followed, with Carter, Buddy, and the deputy right behind us. We all came to a collective screeching halt in the kitchen entryway.

"Oh, my God." I felt as if the air had been sucked out of my lungs. "He's gone."

Misha had not only departed this earth, but his body was nowhere in sight.

Chapter Eight

"IS THIS A TRAINING drill?" Deputy Breaux asked. His face was a mask of confusion. "Or some kind of trick to test my observation skills?"

"Neither," Carter snapped. "There was a body here." He pointed to the spot on the floor where Misha had recently lain. "He was a big guy, at least six foot and well over two hundred fifty pounds would be my guess."

"You're sure he was dead?" Gertie asked.

I spun around to look at her, ready to call her out on her ridiculous question, but I caught my great-aunt's subtle head shake. She wanted me to hold my tongue. I glanced at Fortune, who was being uncharacteristically quiet.

Why was Gertie asking such a ludicrous question? Why wouldn't Fortune immediately confirm that Misha had just been lying here dead not twelve minutes ago? Why did Aunt Ida Belle want me to keep silent? The only reason that made any sense, even remotely, was that they were going to let Carter think that Misha hadn't really been dead.

But hadn't Carter checked Misha's pulse? Wouldn't Buddy confirm that the body he'd found had shown no signs of life? I looked at each of the three women in turn. They were some kind of crazy.

"Of course, I'm sure." Carter's face was growing redder by the moment. "Don't even, *do not even*, think you're going to get away with telling me you didn't see the body that was right here."

"Of course we saw it. We're old, not blind." Aunt Ida Belle's face was impressively impassive. "But I've also been around long enough to tell you this much, stiffs just don't get up and walk away."

"Word," Gertie chimed in. "Did you take a picture of it?"

Carter narrowed his eyes. "No, did you?"

In answer, Gertie shivered. "What kind of a pervert would do something like that?"

I closed my eyes and issued a silent prayer that Gertie would shut up while she was still ahead of the game. Carter looked mad enough to arrest us all.

"Fortune, look at me," Carter ordered.

She turned slowly to face him. Like my great-aunt, Fortune had a face that was readable only when she wanted it to be, so it was near on impossible to know exactly what she was thinking. But I knew she had a thing for Carter, and he for her, which made this a miserable situation for them both.

Leave it to the Sidorov family to mess up the lives of people they didn't even know. Unbelievable.

"Fortune, tell me that you saw the body."

She nodded. "I did."

"You saw that he was dead?"

She hesitated. "I saw him lying there, not moving. But I didn't take his pulse."

"Damn it, Fortune," Carter turned away in disgust.

An uncomfortable silence settled over us. Carter's anger and Fortune's despair were both painfully palpable.

"Um, Carter, don't you think we should do something?"

The deputy's words were the jumpstart Carter needed to snap back into professional mode. He nodded. "Right. Here's what's going to happen. I'm declaring this house a crime scene because a murder occurred here." He paused long enough for one of us to refute that claim, but no one spoke. Apparently satisfied, he continued, "Buddy, you stay here and get these windows replaced. Deputy Breaux will stay with you until the job is done, and then you're going to follow him down to the department and give your statement. If I hear that you've so much as spoken one word to any of these women," he motioned to the four of us, "then I'm throwing your butt in jail and leaving it there. Understand?"

Buddy nodded. "Got it."

"Fortune, gather up Merlin and your things and go stay with Gertie or Ida Belle until I give you the okay to return."

Color returned to Fortune's cheeks in one swift flush. "You're kicking me out of my own house?"

"Damn straight." He stood with his feet planted a good twelve inches apart and his hands on his hips. "If it helps you any, don't think of this as your house. Think of it as a crime scene. If you come back here for any reason, any of you, I swear to God I'll arrest you. If you think I'm kidding, just try me."

I don't know what the ladies were thinking, but I for one was going to take his threat seriously. I had no desire to see the inside of a Sinful, Louisiana jail cell.

"WE NEED TO GO BACK to the house after dark." Aunt Ida Belle handed me a mason jar of sweet tea and sat in the seat beside me. "I want to find out where that body went off to."

We were holed up at Gertie's house, having been banished from Fortune's. I stared down at my sweetened tea. I knew it was a southern tradition, but I would have far preferred a china tea cup filled with unsweetened black tea and a lemon wedge. Never mind the beverage at hand, I just flat out wished I were back in Boston. I'd come to Sinful to hide out while Misha forgot about me. Obviously, things weren't going according to plan.

Poor Misha.

Poor me.

"Snap out of it, Stephanie." Aunt Ida Belle clapped her hands together. "This isn't a pity party. We've got to figure out a game plan."

I turned to look her square in the eye. "What's the game?"

She returned my gaze without so much as blinking. "It's called 'Keep Stephanie St. James Out of Jail.'"

Gertie placed a plate of freshly baked chocolate chip cookies on the table. She sat opposite me. "I'll play. I'm feeling lucky."

That made one of us.

"What about you, Fortune?" my great-aunt asked.

Fortune turned to us, her blue eyes as serious as I'd seen them since I'd arrived in Sinful. "Carter wasn't kidding when he said he'd arrest us if he caught us near the house."

"Then we won't get caught." Gertie took a bite out of a cookie. "Easy peasy."

"I still don't understand what we hope to find at the house," I said.

"Misha," Gertie and Aunt Ida Belle answered in unison.

"He was dead, wasn't he?" I had to ask. I mean, I knew he was dead. I saw his body. He wasn't breathing. He wasn't blinking. But he also wasn't there when we went back into the kitchen. I'll admit that was starting to really creep me out.

"Yes, he was dead. Is dead." Fortune got up and started to pace. Her nervous energy was ricocheting off the walls. "I think he was poisoned."

"What points to poison?" Aunt Ida Belle asked.

"Gut instinct." Fortune shrugged. "I could be wrong, but I don't think I am. The way his features were arrested, almost frozen, could only be caused by a fast-acting poison. That and the fact there were no signs of a struggle or any visible wounds."

There was an intensity to the way that Fortune spoke and moved that seemed at odds with what Aunt Ida Belle had told me about her background. She was a former beauty queen turned librarian, but she reminded me of someone who had a military background. Perhaps her parents had been military. Either way, I wasn't in any position to challenge her hypothesis. Misha had been my first. Corpse, that is.

"Who'd want his dead body?" Gertie asked. "That's what I can't figure out. With mob connections, I get that there might have been a waiting list of people who wanted him dead. But why whisk away the body?"

"I think the real question is, why kill him in Fortune's kitchen?" Aunt Ida Belle got up to pace, too.

Maybe this was the way of southern women when they were puzzling something out. If so, it would only be polite to join in the to and fro, but my knees were still shaky. I glanced at Gertie for a social cue. She grabbed another cookie and proceeded to eat it, apparently not caring that Aunt Ida Belle and Fortune were pacing like two caged lions.

"Misha, or whoever shot out my windows last night, could have easily broken in and killed Stephanie. So it stands to reason that they only wanted to give her a warning."

"I understand why they would want me dead," I said, although the words sounded all wrong once they were out. "If I were out of the picture, I couldn't testify that I heard Misha say he executed someone. But who would want Misha dead?"

Aunt Ida Belle's glance was downright pitying. "You don't know much about the mob, do you, Stephanie, honey?"

"More than I want to, actually." But I took her point. We could work on the assumption that all mobsters had someone who wanted them six feet under. "But why kill him here?"

All three women fixed a knowing look on me while they waited for me to add two plus two. I did and got four. "They wanted to kill him here because someone would eventually make the connection between us." I put my hand to my throat as if doing so could ward off the noose I felt tightening around my neck. "They want to pin it on me."

"Bingo!" Gertie shouted, her fist pumping the air. "There's hope for Miss Prim and Proper yet."

"Can it, Gertie," my great-aunt scolded her. "The kid's a novice. Go easy on her."

"Sorry." Gertie smiled apologetically. "I got carried away."

I tried to keep the shock off of my face. These women gave a whole new meaning to the definition of steel magnolias.

"There's nothing to be gained by going back to the house," Fortune said. "Think about it. No one would bother to move Misha from one room to another, right? They wanted to clear him out of there. If they did, he's long gone. But if they didn't succeed for some reason, the body would have been found by now. It's not like we're going to find Misha under a bush in the backyard. Carter's going to tear my place apart looking for that body."

"Well, we sure as heck aren't going to sit here and wait for someone to come after my great-niece."

"I wasn't suggesting that," Fortune said. "Let's think this through. We were all standing on the porch and we know the body didn't come out that way."

"I could see the inside stairway from where I stood, but no one went up or down," Gertie said. "So they must have used the back door."

"Which would lead straight to the water, which meant someone must have had a boat ready. Someone with the resources to have a boat quiet enough and fast enough to get that body out of there in a matter of minutes, not to mention the manpower to get the job done." Her smile was downright triumphant. "Sound like anyone we know?"

"Whoo hoo!" Gertie stood up and did what I assume was supposed to look like a happy dance, although it actually looked like she was shaking the ants out of her polyester pants. "Good work, girl."

My eyes went to Aunt Ida Belle. Just as I thought, she looked as delighted as her two friends.

"Well, don't stand there, get on the phone and make the call. Tell them we need to see them tonight," she demanded.

"Who?" I asked, not really surprised when no one answered me. I tried again. "Where are we going?"

But it didn't really matter. Wherever they were going, I was going too. There was no way I was going to stay behind and serve as target practice for the Russian mob.

Chapter Nine

WE TUMBLED OUT OF GERTIE'S house and into her Cadillac about ten minutes after Fortune made a mysterious phone call. I didn't know whom she called but it didn't really matter. Aunt Ida Belle, Gertie, and Fortune seemed almost jubilant, which gave me hope that we were now officially on our way to proving my innocence.

I glanced across the street at Carter's house as we piled into the car. Only one small yellow light shone from his front porch. I'd have felt reassured if interior lights had blazed from the inside of his house because that would mean he was off duty. But the darkness unnerved me. Was he sitting at his desk down at the police station putting together a rock solid case against me?

At the very thought of incarceration, my stomach did a funny little flip flop. Well, not so funny, actually. The prospect of jail time terrified me. Of course, I wasn't the one who killed Misha, so I shouldn't technically be worried. Except that I was. What if the Sidorovs decided that framing me for their precious son's murder was the perfect way to punish me? For some very twisted reason, they seemed to be shocked that I didn't want to marry Misha and join their family.

The squeal of the tires as Gertie's Cadillac peeled around a corner shook me from my reverie. I glanced out the window. Not a wise move. The speed at which we were traveling, coupled with the erratic lane changes, left me downright nauseated. I closed my eyes.

"Are you okay, Stephanie?"

I opened one eye and snuck a quick look at Fortune. She was holding on to the back of Gertie's seat as if it were a bucking bronco. Except that this ride wouldn't be over in eight seconds.

"I'm fine," I lied. "I just want to survive the ride."

Fortune smiled. "Gertie always manages to get us where we need to go in one piece. At least so far. That's not a bad record considering how blind she is."

"I heard that." Gertie frowned at us over her shoulder. "Whatever happened to respecting your elders?"

A horn blasted and Aunt Ida Belle leaned across the front seat to jerk the wheel to the right. "Keep looking straight, you old fool. The highway on-ramp is coming up soon."

I closed my eyes again, wishing that I could block the memory of Misha's lifeless body as easily as I blocked out my vision. The Cadillac accelerated at an alarming rate, and my heart-rate did the same. I blew out a deep breath. Eventually this would all be over, both the car ride and the whole Misha mess. One way or the other.

"Fortune?" I still had my eyes closed. Watching Gertie zigzag between semi-trucks was more than I could handle. "Was Misha really dead?"

"Yes," she said without hesitation. "He was as dead as a man could be."

"You're sure?"

"It's the only thing in this whole situation I am sure about," she said. "Misha was stone cold dead. We know that. The rest of the puzzle we're going to have to piece together."

I felt a rush of gratitude toward Fortune, Gertie, and my great-aunt Ida Belle. I was a virtual stranger to all three of them, only loosely connected by bloodline to my great-aunt, and yet they were acting as if my problems were theirs. Yes, they were wild, they were crazy, and their manners were not what I expected from southern ladies, but they were loyal and resourceful. And I was grateful.

A very long fifteen minutes later, the Cadillac slowed from autobahn speed to normal speed and then finally to a bumpy crawl over what felt like a dirt road. I opened my eyes and looked around, but all I saw was blackness. "Where are we?"

"Almost there," my great-aunt said.

Well, that was as clear as bayou mud. But to push for more answers when it was obvious she didn't want to fill me in would be downright rude. I might well be close to losing my mind, but that didn't mean I had to abandon my manners.

Gertie pulled the car to a stop in front of a warehouse. It wasn't exactly rundown, but neither was it particularly inviting. Still, I followed Fortune out of the car without hesitating. We stood in huddle formation in the parking lot.

"I'll do the talking," Aunt Ida Belle said. "Fortune, jump in when you feel you need to. Stephanie, you'd best stay as quiet as possible unless you're asked a question. Answer it as succinctly as possible and don't add any details unless I prompt you to. Don't confess to anything, either. The less you say, the better."

I nodded, although the use of the word "confess" didn't sit comfortably with me. However, this didn't seem the right time to quibble over semantics.

"What about me?" Gertie demanded.

"You keep silent," aunt Ida Belle said. "I don't want to hear a word out of you. Last time we were here you really pushed it with those Bibles and all that crazy 'have you been saved' gibberish."

My eyebrows rose. Now there was a story.

But it wasn't one I was destined to hear right now. Bright floodlights lit up the driveway and a voice called out through the night. "What do youse want?"

I heard Gertie suck in her breath.

"Don't do it, Gertie," Aunt Ida Belle hissed. "Let it go. It's just a word."

"Like hell I will." Gertie's face scrunched into a scowl as she turned to face the building. The lights were too bright for any of us to see anything, but that didn't stop Gertie from shaking her finger in the general direction of the building. "Watch your language, young man. There are southern ladies out here and we don't appreciate your wise guy slang." She took a step toward the warehouse. "'Youse' is not a word. Do not let me hear you use it again."

Fortune shook her head. "Wait for it," she whispered to me. "She just won't leave well enough alone."

Gertie hitched her handbag up onto her shoulder. "Or else," she called out to the grammar offender.

A door creaked open and light from inside the building framed the silhouette of a hulking figure. I'd seen men built in this bulky shape before, and they all worked for the Sidorov family.

"Oh yeah?" the voice shot back. "And I bet you think that 'y'all' is a word? 'Cause it's not."

Gertie lunged forward but Aunt Ida Belle caught her by the arms before she could charge the voice. Fortune took several steps toward the glaring light.

"We're here to see Mr. Hebert," she said. "Please tell him that the ladies he's expecting from Sinful have arrived."

A low guttural growl was our only indication that the hulk was done taunting Gertie. "Which Mr. Hebert?"

"I believe they're both expecting us."

"Wait here." He stepped back into the warehouse and slammed the door shut. He must have flipped off a power switch as well because we were soon back to seeing by moonlight.

"So much for keeping your flap trap shut." Aunt Ida Belle released her hold on Gertie. "What are you trying to do? Encourage the Heberts to put us on their 'shoot on sight' list?"

Gertie shook out her arms like a prizefighter. "I will not sanction the Jersey-fication of our language."

I sympathized with her concerns because I'm also an advocate of proper diction. But an image of myself on trial for murder prompted me to reprioritize. We had a body to find. "Gertie, we can buy this gentleman a dictionary at a later date. Right now I think we should focus on the matter at hand."

She stared at me for a moment before she nodded. "You're right." She reached out and patted my shoulder. "We'll get your boyfriend's body back."

"Boyfriend?" I sucked in a lungful of humid nighttime air. "No, you have it all wrong. Misha's not my boyfriend. I mean, he wasn't my boyfriend. It wasn't like that."

"What was it like?" Fortune asked, her voice gentle. "There must have been something going on if he followed you all the way down here."

I shook my head emphatically. "Believe me, our relationship was strictly professional, at least on my side. Misha had a crush on me, and he was so spoiled that he couldn't fathom not getting what he wanted."

"And he wanted you," Fortune supplied.

I nodded. "His father, Boris Sidorov, believed that Misha had executed someone and that I was a witness." I'd told them all this before. "So if he could force me to marry Misha, then it would kill two birds with one stone." I grimaced at my poor choice of words.

"Right, he thought that you'd be immune from testifying against your husband should this come to trial," Aunt Ida Bella said. "And if you married Misha, Boris' precious little boy would get just what he wanted."

I sighed. "Exactly."

"Was there bad blood between them?" Gertie asked. "Any chance that Boris ordered a hit on his son?"

"Zero. Boris loves all of his sons, especially Misha. He couldn't do anything wrong in his father's eyes."

"So who would want Misha dead?" Gertie asked.

"And who would want to steal his body?" Aunt Ida Belle asked.

"That's what we're about to find out." Fortune motioned to the warehouse with her head. The door was open and the gigantic guard stood in the doorway. "Let's go."

We were granted access to the warehouse and ushered up the stairs to a suite of offices. I looked around as we headed upstairs, but the interior gave me no clue as to what sort of business this was. We stopped in front of a closed door and waited while the guard rapped on the door.

The door swung open and a man of incredibly short stature greeted us with a smile. "Welcome, ladies."

My companions greeted him as we shuffled in. My eyes swept the office and stopped when I saw another man sitting behind a desk. This man was enormous, by far the largest human being I'd ever encountered. He had to weigh five hundred pounds if he weighed one. His black eyes were locked on to me with an unnerving intensity.

"Hello," I said, knowing that it was rude to stare. "I'm Stephanie St. James."

"I know who you are, Miss Prim and Proper."

I blinked in surprise. "How do you know about that?"

"I am an avid reader of your column." He gestured to the other man in the room. "It's safe to say that we have both learned quite a bit about etiquette from you."

I was flattered, I'll admit it. "Thank you. That's so kind of you to say."

He pointed to a chair in front of his desk. "Sit. We have to talk."

I sat.

His eyes were locked onto mine. "I believe I have something you might be looking for."

Chapter Ten

"BUT FIRST, ALLOW ME to introduce myself," the man said. "I'm Big."

My eyes widened. That was certainly stating the obvious.

"I'm Big Hebert and this is my son, Little." He motioned for the smaller man to come forward and greet me.

After we shook hands, Little went to stand behind his father. Gertie, Ida Belle, and Fortune gathered behind my chair. My heart beat in my chest at four times its normal rate. I'd never witnessed a sit-down before, let alone participated in one.

Something in the way that Big held court reminded me of Boris Sidorov. He spoke with an air of authority, and there was an inherent expectation in his manner that he would be obeyed. The bulky guards outside the door were another not so subtle tip-off.

It was obvious Big Hebert had mob connections. So why were we here?

"You mentioned that you have something of mine?" I asked.

Big shook his head. "No, I said I have something you might be looking for."

I swore, softly and in French, but still I swore. It was hardly a ladylike reaction, but I have to think that under these circumstances, it could be excused. At least that's what I would tell my dear readers. The truth was, I swore because I felt like the quicksand went from my knees to my waist. I was sinking fast.

"Something I might be looking for?" I repeated, thinking it wise to tap dance around Misha's name.

Big nodded. "I'm referring to a certain *someone*." He laid extra emphasis on the last word. So Big could tap dance too. This shouldn't surprise me, not considering his line of work.

"He means Misha," Gertie blurted out, plowing in where angels knew not to tread.

Again, Big nodded. "He's downstairs."

My hand went to my throat and I clutched my pearls as if they were a lifeline. "You mean, his body is downstairs?"

"It is." Big gave me a moment to compose myself before he continued. "I can confirm that Mr. Sidorov has met with an untimely passing. The question now becomes how to dispose of his body. I thought of you, naturally."

Naturally.

"Wait," Fortune spoke before I could think of what to say. "Let's back this up. How did you get Misha's body out of my kitchen so quickly?"

"Back up even further. How did you know he died?" Gertie demanded.

Big held his hands out in front of him, palms facing upward. His shrug was elegant. "I have sources."

"Buddy McBride," I said aloud. It made sense, in an odd sort of way. Buddy found the body, and even though he told Fortune that he called her immediately after calling the police, he could have contacted the Heberts before anyone else. But why would he? He hardly seemed like the type to be a mob informant. However, maybe that worked in his favor because no one would suspect he was on the take just by looking at him. "Why would you care what happened to Misha?"

Gertie waved her hands wildly. "Hold up, now. Are you telling me that Buddy McBride, poor, clueless, always trying to keep up Buddy, works for you?"

"We're not at liberty to discuss that with you ladies, and you're certainly not at liberty to discuss it with anyone else," Little said. "Do we understand each other?"

We nodded our agreement.

"Good. Now, it doesn't matter precisely when we got the call, but there's a body downstairs that needs to be removed from our premises. Pronto."

"But I don't want Misha's body," I blurted out. "You took it, you keep it."

Big's eyebrows rose. "Now, Miss Prim and Proper, that hardly strikes me as an appropriate response after we've done you a favor."

"Some favor." I could hear how ill-mannered I sounded, but that was the least of my problems right now. "I didn't want Misha when he was alive. I certainly don't want him now."

Big shook his head ruefully, as if he were disappointed in me. He turned his attention to my great-aunt. "As the senior stateswoman in the group, I assume you can understand why we need you to remove the body. Tonight."

Aunt Ida Belle put a hand on my shoulder, which I took as a warning to be silent and trust she knew what she was doing. "We're certainly open to considering that, but we need to know why you swooped in and took the body in the first place. And as you reminded us, so shall I remind you, time's a'wastin.'"

Big sat back and somehow managed to lace his fingers together over his corpulent stomach. "It came to our attention, and please don't ask how because I won't tell you, that Misha Sidorov was in town looking for your great-niece. It also came to our attention that his older brother, Vladimir, followed him down here and arranged to have Misha poisoned. Seeing as how my son and I are fans of Miss St. James, the least we could do was move the body. This gave us time to warn her because Deputy LeBlanc can't arrest her for murder without a victim. We've also had the opportunity to tip off Boris Sidorov that Mikhail was killed. Now that you know the stakes, our work is done."

Vladimir? I shuddered. I'd never liked Misha's oldest brother. In fact, I found him downright creepy. He'd always struck me as someone with a cruel side. But to murder his own brother? I couldn't find the words to describe how heinous that was. "And why here in Sinful? Couldn't he have done that in Boston and left us out of it?"

Big looked at Little, his amusement clear. "She's a real innocent, this one."

Little nodded his agreement.

I swiveled around to look at my companions. They wore pitying expressions.

"Stephanie, we discussed this back at my house, remember?" Gertie asked.

"Yes, but it didn't sound right back at the house and it still doesn't. It's too far-fetched."

"You need to believe us, Stephanie," Fortune said. "We've all come to the same conclusion. Think it through. It makes sense. We can't know for sure, but the most obvious reason that Vladimir would kill Misha here in Sinful is so that a connection would eventually be made between you and Misha."

"A connection?"

"Oh, Lawdy Miss Clawdy, just spell it out for her," Gertie all but shouted.

"Stephanie," my great-aunt said, her voice far more in control than Gertie's, "Vladimir Sidorov wants to pin his brother's murder on you. He set it up to look like Misha followed you here and you killed him. Even the method of murder points to you."

I frowned. "It does?"

Fortune nodded. "It does. If you were going to kill someone, how would you do it?"

"I've never thought about it," I replied, more than a little offended.

"Aw, come on. Confess." Gertie gave my shoulder a playful punch. "We've all thought about murdering someone." She looked around for support. "Haven't we?"

To a one, each person nodded their agreement. I had the most uncomfortable feeling that several of the people I was sitting with probably had committed a murder. I was so out of my element with this crowd. "Well, I guess I'd smother someone with a soft pillow while they were sleeping. Poison would work, too, if it were fast acting."

My great-aunt patted my shoulder. "Good girl."

"So you can see why people would be far more likely to believe that you'd poison Misha rather than gun him down in cold blood," Fortune said.

The mention of guns sparked a question in my mind. What did the Heberts know about the shooting at Fortune's house? I asked them.

"Ah, yes, we heard about that," Big said. "Such a shame."

Little nodded his agreement. "Quite regrettable."

"Did you have anything to do with the shooting?"

I could have sworn that Big's eyes narrowed just the tiniest bit. Not surprisingly, he didn't like being challenged.

Well, I didn't like being framed for a murder I didn't commit.

"I will make an allowance for your confusion," Big said. "And, just for the record, I'll state the obvious. We had nothing to do with the shooting."

"But why would anyone shoot up Fortune's kitchen like that?" I persisted. "Someone could have gotten hurt."

Little's smile was indulgent. "Rest assured, whoever orchestrated the shooting didn't want to cause injuries. If they had, one or all of you ladies wouldn't be sitting here today. No, my guess would be that they simply wanted to establish your presence in Sinful."

"Establish my presence?" It sounded like English but I had no idea what he meant.

"Your friends in law enforcement certainly learned of it, didn't they? Deputy LeBlanc came out and connected you with the ensuing chaos. You're now on the sheriff's radar. Ergo, their mission was accomplished."

I got to my feet. I'd heard all I wanted to hear. My head was about to burst. "Thank you both for the explanation, but I'll decline your offer to release Misha's body to me. I want nothing to do with it."

Big leaned forward. "Your wishes are irrelevant, Miss St. James. I understand if you're still too confused to thank us properly for removing Misha's body, but that doesn't change the fact that it's now time for you to escort your former associate to the morgue."

"Escort?" Gertie asked. "You've got a hearse parked somewhere around here?"

Little shook his head. "No, but we've got an airboat. As we speak, our associates are loading the body onto it and it will carry Misha down the bayou. The plan is for you and your friends to meet the boat at the mortuary. We'll unload the body onto a gurney for you but our involvement ends there."

"So all we have to do is break into the mortuary and get the body inside?" Gertie asked. "That's do-able."

Big smile's was enigmatic. "Yes, it is. By tomorrow morning, this will be the sheriff's problem. Not yours. Not ours."

"But what if we get caught with Misha's body?" I could see flashing red and blue police lights in my mind's eye and I could hear the clink of the jail cell door closing behind me. "The police will think we killed Misha."

"Very true." Big motioned to his hulking associate to open the doors. It was clear the interview was over. "So I suggest you don't get caught."

Chapter Eleven

WE CLIMBED BACK INTO Gertie's Cadillac and began the trek back to Sinful. My mind was awhirl with jumbled thoughts as we bumped along the darkened back roads. I desperately wanted someone to reassure me that the Heberts were flat out crazy and we were simply going to ignore them.

But no one said a word.

Once we were on the highway, I decided I might as well be the one to initiate the discussion. Somebody had to say something. Besides, perhaps conversation would distract Gertie enough that she'd stay within twenty miles of the speed limit. "So Big and Little certainly were talking crazy back there, weren't they?"

Still, no one said anything. I was quickly learning that silence wasn't golden with these ladies. It was downright dangerous, because it meant they were hatching a plan. One I doubted I was going to like.

"I have an idea," I tried again. "Why don't we call the sheriff's office and leave an anonymous tip telling them where Misha's body is? That way they can retrieve it and send it home."

"No way, no how," Gertie said over her shoulder.

"Why?"

"Because ticking off the Heberts is a very bad idea."

"Are you afraid of them?"

Aunt Ida Belle turned to look at me. In the darkness I could only see enough of her face to see that she wasn't pleased by my question. "Of course not. But we're not fools, and we have a healthy respect for their position in the community. For their connections, if you will. Besides, I'm thinking that maybe their plan isn't so very farfetched."

"I'm thinking the same thing," Fortune concurred.

I stared at them. "I'm thinking that you're both crazy."

"We've been accused of worse." Gertie flashed me a thumbs up from the front seat.

Well, at least I hadn't offended her.

"I'm so confused," I said. "Why would Mr. Hebert swoop in and 'help' by taking Misha's body but now refuse to 'help' return it?"

"He accomplished what he wanted by taking the body. He was able to stick it to the Sidorovs by delivering the news of Misha's death, and he thought he was helping you. But now he's ready to wash his hands of the whole affair." Fortune's voice was calm and thoughtful, but it didn't escape my notice that she was clinging to the car door as if her life depended on it. "Big might well say that he took Misha as a favor to you so that you wouldn't be incriminated, but there's more to it than that. There always is with people like the Heberts."

This little lesson I'd learned courtesy of the Sidorovs. "So what was in it for him?"

Fortune shrugged. "Who knows? Maybe a cat and mouse game with the Sidorovs? Can you imagine how Vladimir reacted to the news that the police didn't find his brother's body? He's probably having fits."

Yeah, fits of rage that would be directed at me once he found me. I suddenly wished Gertie could keep driving on the highway, right past the Sinful exit. "So why can't Mr. Hebert just make the body disappear? He's probably slowed people down from connecting me to Misha, but once the body's found and identified, someone can still finger me for the murder."

"Whoo hoo, listen to your niece, Ida Belle," Gertie sounded downright gleeful. "'Finger me for the murder'. She's really picking up the lingo."

But Aunt Ida Belle didn't appear to share any of Gertie's delight. "My niece is still in the hot seat. Vladimir is going to need somewhere to direct his anger when he sees that his plan's been thwarted. Stephanie's gonna be his target. She's in worse trouble now than if Carter had found the body on the kitchen floor."

"Not necessarily," Fortune said. "I don't think it's very sporting of Big and Little to just dump the body on us, but we can still turn this to our advantage."

"How?" I asked.

"We get the body back into the morgue, and we leave a note with it. So when the mortician calls Carter about the body that mysteriously showed up overnight, they can pass along the contact information for Vladimir."

Aunt Ida Belle nodded. "That puts Vladimir in the line of fire of police questioning. Good. Hopefully, he won't have a ready alibi."

"He will," I said. "The Sidorovs aren't stupid. Vladimir will have his tracks covered."

"And we'll cover yours," Gertie said. "After all, we haven't let you out of our sight since you arrived in Sinful, so you can't have been the one to poison Misha. We'll be your alibi."

"I don't want to sound rude, or ungrateful, but I think you're all underestimating Misha's family."

"And I think you're underestimating us," Aunt Ida Belle said. "We've got this covered."

Fortune and Gertie appeared to be in complete agreement. I kept my thousand and one concerns and objections to myself, and didn't say anything.

Gertie turned off the highway and headed toward Sinful. I still wasn't familiar with the layout of the town, especially in the dark, but it seemed we were heading in a different direction than we'd gone before.

"Where are we going?" I asked, not sure I really wanted to hear the answer.

"The morgue," Gertie answered. She glanced in the rear-view mirror and must have seen the shock on my face. "Now, don't you worry about a thing. We'll zip in, recover Misha's body, slip him into the morgue with a note, and be back home in our flannel pajamas in no time. It'll be smooth sailing."

Smooth sailing? Funny, because I had a sinking feeling that we were about to go down with the ship.

FONTENOT'S MORTUARY and Memorial Chapel sat on the very edge of Sinful's town limits, almost as if it wanted to keep a respectful distance from the part of town where the living spent their days. The parking lot was dark and the premises appeared to be deserted.

Gertie parked in a wooded lot next to the mortuary so that her car wouldn't be visible to anyone passing by. She backed in, she told us, so that we could make a quick get-away.

"Why don't we go back to the house and talk about this?" I half asked, half pleaded.

"Whose house?" Aunt Ida Belle took off her seatbelt and turned around to face me. "Fortune's house that was shot up? Or

Gertie's, where likely Carter is sitting looking out his window waiting for us to come home so that he can watch our every movement?"

"Why not your house?"

I could see that she was trying to keep her cool. She really was. She spoke as patiently as I'd ever heard her. "Because I'd put money on it that the Sidorovs know you're likely to show up there eventually. If they followed you to Sinful, they know that you're my niece. Running into Vladimir or any of his goons isn't going to get us any closer to getting you off the hook."

"We're here now, so let's get our plan straight," Fortune said.

I shot a curious glance at her. For an ex-beauty queen and a librarian, she certainly had a take-charge, commanding personality. Something didn't jibe.

"Stephanie, why don't you stay here with the car while Ida Belle and I go take a look around back?" she asked.

"What about me?" Gertie demanded.

"You're not getting out of this car," Aunt Ida Belle told her. "If you do, I just know that this will somehow turn into the Great Coffin Fiasco."

Gertie glared at my great-aunt. "You've been at the center of a few fiascos in your day, Ida Belle."

"True, but not nearly a fraction of the ones you have."

Fortune held up both hands. "Stop. You two can duke this out later. If Big really did send a boat down the bayou, it should be docking around back about now. No one's going to be very happy if we keep them waiting."

Ida Belle slid out of the front seat and quietly closed the door. She motioned for me to follow her. "I want my niece with us. If this is a trap, we can't leave her just sitting here ripe for the picking."

I didn't wait for Fortune to respond. I opened my door and got out. As much as I liked Gertie, my gut instinct told me that I'd be safer with Fortune and my aunt.

Gertie slouched down in the driver's seat. "Fine. Go have fun without me. I'll just sit here wasting away to nothing. An old woman left all alone...."

I watched as aunt Ida Belle and Fortune exchanged glances. I don't know what unspoken agreement passed between them, but without so much as a by-your-leave they started out toward the mortuary parking lot. I gave Gertie an apologetic shrug and hurried after them.

We kept to the darkened perimeter of the property. I did my best to make my way through the brush as quietly as they did, but I was sure the sound of my galloping heart beat could wake the dead. Not a very comforting thought this close to a mortuary.

I smelled the bayou before I saw it. I can't think of any way to describe it except to say that it redefined the word "swampy" in my mind. The night air was thick and heavy. A cadre of insects and critters created a symphony of noises that I'd never heard in Boston. Stars twinkled in the nighttime sky as if they were laughing at our folly.

Fortune stopped and held up a hand. She pointed to a dock behind the mortuary. The shadow of an airboat was barely visible. If we weren't looking for it, we'd easily have missed it.

"It looks like they've got Misha," Fortune whispered.

"Or his coffin anyway," Aunt Ida Belle said.

The thought of Misha's lifeless body boxed up like that made me ill. Literally. I turned away and lost my lunch as discreetly as I could. Thankfully, I always carry a lace-trimmed handkerchief. "I can't do this," I said after I blotted my lips. "We shouldn't be here."

Aunt Ida Belle's hand closed around my wrist. "But we are, and we're going through with this." She then dropped her bombshell. "Stephanie, I think it would be downright rude of you not to accept our help."

Ouch. She really knew how to deal a blow. We stared at each other for a long moment.

"You're right, Aunt Ida Belle. Please accept my apologies." I squared my shoulders and lifted my head high. "I'm ready."

Fortune pointed in the direction of the boat. "You're not the only one."

Two moving figures, so large they had to be Big and Little's henchmen, stood on the dock, a gurney with a coffin on it alongside them.

"Let's roll," Fortune whispered over her shoulder as she began to move.

We crept along the side of the property until we were within a stone's throw of the men. They appeared unaware of our approach.

"Where the hell are they?" the first one growled. "Big's going to be spitting mad if we have to bring the stiff back to the warehouse."

Stiff? I took great umbrage to that. Misha, every law-breaking, narcissistic ounce of him, was dead and should be spoken of with at least a modicum of respect. My fear of the Sidorovs faded as my temper flared. I stepped out onto the paved lot. "I'll ask you not to speak of that poor deceased gentleman in such a disparaging tone."

Both men jumped, clearly startled at the sound of my voice. I felt a bit smug at the realization that they obviously hadn't heard us approach. Good. I had their full attention. It struck me as the perfect time for a lesson on speaking respectfully of the dead. I marched over to stand in front of them. "The man in the coffin, Mikhail Sidorov, has now gone to meet his maker. It's a fate that awaits us all, including the both of you." It was dark so I wasn't able to clearly read their expressions, but I knew they were looking at me.

"Look, lady, we don't need no lecture—" one of the goons began, but I held up my hand to stop him right there. Gertie certainly would have if she'd been here to hear his use of a double negative.

"Yes, you are correct, I am a lady. However, you do not have the right to address me in such a disrespectful tone of voice. Is that clear?"

Instead of answering, they both took a step backward, somehow managing to bump into each other as they did so.

"Gentleman, I'm not certain what part of this great nation you both hail from, but I can't imagine that where you were raised it was polite to ignore a lady's question." I was just warming up. I'd missed working directly with clients. There was nothing like bringing a sense of propriety to individuals unfortunate enough not to have been raised properly to warm my heart. "I'm not sure what direct instructions Mr. Hebert gave you—"

"He told us to dump the body and hightail it back when you all showed up," the larger of the two said. "So that's what we're gonna do."

"Not so fast." I pointed to the back door of the mortuary. There were five concrete steps leading up to a not particularly wide door. "The least you can do is open that door for us. And please do not pretend that you don't know how to pick a lock. I know better."

"We're not sticking around to help, lady," hulk number one said. He looked at his associate and jerked his head in the direction of their boat. The other man nodded and they broke out into a trot.

They jumped onto their airboat and started it up before I could catch my breath.

"Wait," I called after them, panic rising in my chest. "Come back here. We need your help." But I was speaking to their boat's wake as they sped out of sight.

Aunt Ida Belle came to stand behind me. She laid a comforting hand on my shoulder. "Let it go, child. We can manage this without them."

"We need to go and check the lock, so just wait here for a minute. And Stephanie, your aunt's right," Fortune said, her voice resolute. "We can do this ourselves."

Like heck we could. They were seriously overestimating our abilities, and I couldn't take it anymore. I whirled around to confront them. Unfortunately, I moved so quickly that I stumbled and bumped into the gurney that held Misha's coffin.

Transfixed, I watched in horror as the gurney began to roll in the direction of the bayou's bank. I struggled to speak, but the words were stuck in my throat. Only a strangled cry came out.

"Hush, Stephanie," my great-aunt called out from the mortuary steps. "Just keep watch while we work on this lock."

I kept watch all right. I watched as the gurney headed straight for the bayou. I watched as one of the wheels got caught on a rock and it jerked sideways. I watched as the coffin slid straight off the back and down the embankment.

And then I watched in horror as Misha Sidorov's coffin sank into the Louisiana bayou.

Chapter Twelve

I STILL HADN'T MANAGED to speak when I heard squealing tires in the front parking lot, followed by the sound of a car's horn.

Fortune and Aunt Ida Belle ran down the steps and joined me.

"I'll go see what that crazy Gertie wants." Aunt Ida Belle sprinted off in the direction of the Cadillac.

Fortune frowned as she surveyed the spot where we stood. "Where's the coffin?"

I swallowed hard and pointed toward the water.

I winced at Fortune's sharp intake of breath.

Her eyes were wide. "What happened?"

I opened my mouth to answer, but Aunt Ida Belle came jogging back to where we waited before I could manage a single world.

"We've got to clear out now," she said, looking back over her shoulder. "Carter's on his way over here. Myrtle just called Gertie's cell. A call came into the station about suspicious activity near the mortuary. She called him and then Gertie. Let's go."

My feet were rooted to the spot. I pointed toward the empty gurney. "Misha." It came out as a barely audible squeak.

Aunt Ida Belle's eyes grew wide and she gasped. "Where's the coffin?"

"We don't have time to explain." Fortune gave me a tiny shove in the direction of my great-aunt. "Just get her in the car and I'll be right behind you. Go."

This was all Aunt Ida Belle needed to hear. She grabbed my arm and dragged me along beside her, not letting go until we reached the Cadillac. She yanked open the door and shoved me in the backseat.

"Where's Fortune?" Gertie demanded.

"I'm right here," Fortune ran up and dove in beside me, almost as if she'd done it a dozen times before. "Go."

Gertie needed no further inducement. Her lead foot hit the gas pedal and the Cadillac tore out of the parking lot.

"Go east," Ida Belle shouted as we neared the entrance. "Carter's most likely to come from the west."

Fortune toppled into my lap as Gertie whipped around the corner. I helped her sit back up. "Are you okay?"

She nodded. "You?"

I shook my head vigorously. No. I was as far from okay as a person could be. "Misha." It was all I could say. The image of his coffin hitting the water and disappearing from sight was tattooed into my brain. It was never going to go away.

"What about him?" Gertie asked.

I moaned.

"What the hell happened back there?" Ida Belle frowned at me as if I were a naughty school girl rather than a woman traumatized. "Misha's dead. You're going to have to accept that."

Yeah, the idea was really starting to sink in.

"We can talk once we get to Gertie's house," Fortune said. She turned to look out the back window. "No sign of any headlights behind us, so I think we've dodged Carter."

"For now." Aunt Ida Belle reached over and tapped Gertie's shoulder. "Slow down. We don't need anyone calling the police because they've spotted us tearing through town."

Gertie immediately brought down her speed to a crawl.

"Oh, for cryin' out loud, go thirty miles an hour, you old fool," Aunt Ida Belle snapped. "You can't ever just fly under the radar, can you?"

"Only sissies fly under the radar." Gertie drove on through the quiet streets at exactly thirty miles an hour.

I only wished my heart rate would slow down to the same steady pace. I couldn't understand how my companions appeared to recover from adrenaline rushes the way normal people recovered from a sneeze. These women moved fast, talked fast, lied quickly, and appeared to take it all in stride as if it were their normal. Which was a very scary thought.

Gertie pulled into her driveway and switched off the engine. "Just another fun night on the town with the girls."

Aunt Ida Belle was already halfway up to the front door. "Tell that to Carter when he gets here. See how far that story gets you."

Once inside, we all scurried to create the illusion that we'd been home for a good part of the evening. I washed up, changed into my pink nightgown with the lace collar, slipped on the matching robe, and slid my very tired feet into a pair of quilted satin house slippers. I left my pearls on. At this point, I wore them more for comfort than for fashion. I needed the sense of security they provided. The vision of Misha's coffin slipping away replayed itself continuously in my mind.

I was tempted to climb into bed and pull the blankets over my head, but I heard my aunt calling me.

"There you are," she said when I stepped into the living room. "I know it's been a rough night. How about a drink?"

The smell of freshly brewed coffee wafted toward me. I smiled gratefully as I sank into an overstuffed chair. "Thank you. I take my coffee with cream and one lump of sugar."

But instead of a coffee cup, I was offered a University of Louisiana shot glass. I wasn't ill-mannered enough to refuse, even if it wasn't the drink I'd had in mind. Still, I had to ask one question. "It's not Russian vodka, is it?"

"Nope, it's good old American Jack Daniels whiskey." Aunt Ida Belle poured a measure of amber liquid into the tiny glass. "Drink up."

I did. And then I coughed, wheezed, and gasped for air as she poured me a refill.

"Tell us what happened, Stephanie. We don't have much time," Fortune said. "Carter's going to come around here any moment and we all need to be on the same page."

"Did you get the body inside the morgue?" Gertie asked. She laughed and slapped her knee. "Can't you imagine old Tipsy's face tomorrow morning when she opens up shop?"

"Who is Tipsy?" I asked.

"Tipsy Fontenot is Sinful's mortician," my great-aunt explained. "Her name's actually Heidi, but she's tipsy so much of the time that the nickname stuck."

"Well, drunk or sober, she's not going to find Misha's coffin inside of the mortuary tomorrow morning, or any other morning," I said.

Gertie's eyes grew wide in her wrinkled face. "You left him in the back parking lot?"

All eyes were on me. I had to tell them. "No, he's not there. He, well, I stumbled, you see, and accidentally knocked into the gurney. I didn't hit it hard, but I guess I jostled it enough that it began to move. To roll. And then..." I took another shot of liquid courage before continuing "...and then, Misha slipped into the water." I delivered the last five words in such a rush that at first I couldn't tell if Aunt Ida Belle and Gertie understood me.

"Misha's coffin is floating down the bayou?" Gertie asked. "Just like baby Moses?"

I shook my head from side to side. "Not floating, no. He sank."

"I pushed the gurney in and it sank, too," Fortune added. "Carter won't find anything that leads back to us when he takes a look around Fontenot's place. There's no evidence, still no body."

"Misha's in a watery grave," I barely managed to choke out.

"Lord above," Gertie said after a long moment of silence. "It's a good thing I wasn't there, I'd have been blamed."

"No, it's all my fault." I felt my cheeks flame. "Everything is." I don't know if it was the Jack Daniels talking or if my moral compass had finally locked in on the right thing to do, but enough was enough. "I'm going to confess."

"Not dressed like that, you're not," Aunt Ida Belle said. "Now, listen, Stephanie. I know you were raised up north, but part of your roots are southern. Let me tell you something about southern women, we don't fall to our knees when the earth below us shifts."

"That's right," Gertie chimed in. "We don't throw in the towel when the other team is wiping the floor with us. We stand tall. We stand strong."

I looked at Fortune, but she shrugged apologetically. "Yankee born and bred, sorry."

This had to be a nightmare. I lifted up the sleeve of my robe and pinched myself. Hard.

"Bless her heart," Gertie said. "Ida Belle, tell her this isn't a bad dream."

Aunt Ida Belle's frown was ferocious. "She knows that. She's going to do the right thing, aren't you, Stephanie?"

"Right thing?" I repeated. "I'm not even sure I know what that is anymore."

"Well, then, I'll tell you. You're going to lie through your pretty white teeth and help us keep the lid on this whole mess until we can figure out a way to put the screws to Vladimir Sidorov."

The lights from a large vehicle shone through the living room window blinds as it pulled into the driveway. The sound of a slamming door was followed by a loud pounding on Gertie's front door.

Carter was here.

Ida Belle got to her feet. "Now mind you do the right thing, child. Lie like our lives depend on it."

Chapter Thirteen

CARTER LEBLANC STRODE into Gertie's living room, his face six shades of red. "Where have y'all been?"

"Depends on when you're talking about," Gertie said. "You know that Ida Belle and I went to Florida two years ago, and of course you know we both served in Vietnam—"

"Cut the crap, Gertie. You know I meant tonight." He looked from one of us to the other, his gaze lingering the longest on Fortune's face, but he eventually zeroed in on me. "Where were you tonight, Miss St. James?"

I gulped.

"I want the truth." His eyes bore into me like they were drilling holes into my skull.

"Out." It was the best I could manage under some very difficult circumstances. Carter wanted the truth. The girls wanted me to lie. The only way to walk this tightrope was to be as creative with the truth as I possibly could. "We went for a drive. I wanted to see downtown Sinful at night."

"You heard my niece, Carter. She said we were out, and we were out. Trust me, she's a terrible liar."

"A few weeks with you three ought to take care of that little problem." Carter crossed his arms over his chest.

"Quit acting like we're strangers you're here to interrogate," Aunt Ida Belle chided him. "Sit down and have a cup of coffee with us. You can tell us what has you all riled up."

Carter didn't sit. He didn't even blink. I had to think this wasn't a good sign.

"Fortune, are you going to toe the party line here or are you going to tell me the truth about where you've been tonight?"

I felt for Fortune. I really did. She might think she was hiding her feelings for the deputy sheriff, but she most certainly was not. Her dismay was clear for all to see. This wasn't fair. It wasn't right. And I couldn't just sit by and let their relationship suffer because of my problems.

"Deputy LeBlanc," I said. "I believe that you came here to see me, so please direct your questions directly to me. Fortune doesn't answer for me. Neither does my great-aunt or Gertie."

This succeeded in redirecting his attention from Fortune onto me. His eyes locked onto mine. "Where is the body that was on Fortune's kitchen floor this morning?"

I took a deep breath. Here was a chance to step out in truth. To be righteous. To be the woman I wanted to be. "At the bottom of the bayou."

"Aw, damn, I don't know why I bother asking any of you anything." Carter's face registered his disgust. "It's just one lie after another."

"No, I'm telling you—" I began, but Aunt Ida Belle leaned into me and pinched my arm. Hard. I shut up. I couldn't risk another pinch. Not after the night I'd had.

Gertie came to stand in front of me. "Well, Carter, if you're not going to accept our invitation to sit and have a cup of coffee like the southern gentleman that I thought your mama raised you to be, then you'd best hit the road."

Carter didn't move. "I'm not done here. I've got Celia and the big brass breathing down my neck. I've got an eyewitness who reported a body, but I don't have a corpse. Worst of all, I've got the three of you between me and the truth. Let me assure you, I've had enough of this nonsense. It ends now."

Something in his tone gave me the chills.

He reached into his shirt pocket and pulled out a small, clear plastic bag. "Can you identify this by any chance, Miss St. James?"

Fortune, Aunt Ida Belle, and Gertie all leaned forward to peer into the bag. I didn't have to. I knew what was in there. It was my handkerchief. I recognized the lace trim. I must have dropped it near Fontenot's Mortuary after I cleaned my face with it in the wooded area by the parking lot.

"Cotton and lace, big deal." Gertie's tone was disdainful. "That could belong to any woman here in Sinful. Well, except Celia." She chuckled. "I doubt our fair wanna-be mayor has the good manners to...."

And there she stumbled. At the word "manners" Carter knew he had me. I could see the flash of satisfaction in his eyes.

"We're done here," my great-aunt announced. "Carter, you either arrest my niece or you leave this house and don't come back until you can speak to us in a more civil manner."

Carter called her bluff. He reached into his back pocket and pulled out a set of handcuffs. He held them up. "What's it going to be, Miss St. James?"

"Carter," Fortune's voice sounded strained. "Please. Don't do this. Stephanie is innocent of any wrongdoing. She's not capable of—"

"Capable of what?" He interrupted her, his tone clipped. "Finish your sentence, Fortune. She's not capable of what exactly?"

Poor Fortune looked like a deer caught in the headlights of an oncoming big rig. Gertie looked equally frozen, and Aunt Ida Belle was pale, definitely not a natural shade for her. A rush of affection for these women washed over me. I had a good amount of empathy for Carter, it can't be fun to play the bad guy. I also felt more than a little indignation that the Sidorovs had me between a rock and a hard place.

Or so they thought.

"Deputy LeBlanc, I can answer every question you have. I can tell you who the dead man is and precisely where his body's located. Not only that, I can lead you straight to the murderer."

His eyes narrowed. "Do I sense a 'but' coming?"

Smart man. I nodded. "I'll tell you everything you want to know and more, but I need to be on the outside. That means you have to agree not to arrest me."

He studied me carefully for several moments. "Why should I trust you?"

"The company I keep should vouch for me." I gestured toward Fortune, Gertie and Aunt Ida Belle with an open hand. Despite my exceedingly high stress levels, I still wasn't about to point at them. That would be shockingly rude. "I don't expect you to trust me when I'm a virtual stranger. But you know these women. Fundamentally, they're honest, law-abiding, upstanding citizens. Deep down, you know that."

"They're good people. I'll give you that." Carter slipped his handcuffs back into his pocket. "Okay, I agree not to arrest you for obstruction of justice tonight, but that's the most I'll promise."

"I'm going to need you to promise that you'll give me back up when we set a trap for the murderer."

He closed his eyes for a swift moment. "You're as cagey as the rest of these women." He held out his hand. "I accept your terms."

More than a little relieved, I shook on our agreement. Now came the hard part.

To save myself, I had to nail Vladimir Sidorov to the wall.

Chapter Fourteen

"NYET."

I took a deep breath to steady my nerves. I needed to sound in control and a hundred times calmer than I actually felt. I shifted my cell phone to my other ear. "I'm losing patience with you, Vladimir," I said. In reality I was losing my nerve, but he didn't need to know that. A quick glance at Fortune, Gertie, and Aunt Ida Belle reminded me to be tough. Or at least act like it. "I'll repeat myself for the last time. You either meet me at Fortune's house tonight at eight o'clock or I call your father to tell him that it was you who murdered your brother."

I held the phone away from my ear as a stream of Russian curse words filled the air. The vehemence with which Vladimir swore left little need to translate his words. He was flat out enraged. With me.

"Is that a yes or a no, Vladimir?"

Gertie flashed me a double thumbs up. I'm glad one of us was enjoying ourselves.

"I call this bullshit," Vladimir said, his accent so strong it sounded like he said bull-sheet. "My father knows you killed his precious little Mikhail."

"He only believes that because he hasn't seen the proof I have that you're the one responsible for your brother's murder. And I'll thank you not to swear in a lady's presence."

The ensuing explosion of curse words sounded even more venomous than the one before. Misha's brother really needed to work on improving his vocabulary. Perhaps a long stint in prison would give him the time for that little project.

Aunt Ida Belle made a circular motion to indicate that I should wrap up the call, which was fine with me.

"Be there at eight o'clock, Vladimir, or you'll be hearing from your father shortly afterward." I ended the call and dropped the phone onto the coffee table. After this was all over, I wanted a new phone. One that hadn't been exposed to toxic Russian verbiage.

"Good job," Fortune said. She paced the length of Gertie's living room. I could tell she was worried. Her words were encouraging, but her expression made it clear that she didn't think I could pull off tricking Misha's brother into a confession.

Well, that made two of us. But what choice did I have now? None so far as I could see. Someone was going down the river...I shuddered at my own poor choice of phrase...someone was going to take the rap for Misha's murder, and it wasn't going to be me.

I couldn't face life in prison. I'd have to give up my pearls. I'd have to give away my precious cat. I'd have to wear an orange jumpsuit. That thought alone was too much to bear. I've found that pastels flatter my skin tone and brunette hair so much better than bright colors.

And then there was my work. How would Miss Prim and Proper fare while incarcerated? I'm sure I would find no shortage of potential clients in prison, but I wanted more opportunities and challenges than providing lessons on the polite way to eat with a dull plastic spoon or the etiquette of group showers. Oh, no, prison life was not for me.

"I can do this." I said the words aloud, as much to convince myself as my companions.

Aunt Ida Belle patted my hand. "Of course you can, Stephanie."

Gertie, doubtless made as uncomfortable as I was by my aunt's blatant lie, jumped to her feet. "I'm starving. Who else wants to head to Francine's for a late lunch?"

"Count me in," I said. I could use a vanilla milkshake right about now. Plus, I didn't think I could take another six hours of sitting around watching the others watch me. Carter was meeting us at seven so I could get wired and we could go over the plan again. But that was hours away. I needed a distraction now. "Let me just tidy up."

I returned a few minutes later smartly turned out in a white eyelet sleeveless dress with a lilac shantung silk handbag and shoes. Mob or no mob, I wasn't going to start dressing in t-shirts and yoga pants.

When I suggested we walk to Francine's instead of racing up there in Gertie's Cadillac, I was quickly vetoed. Aunt Ida Belle felt we weren't protected enough if we were walking, Fortune agreed we'd be too vulnerable, and Gertie, well, Gertie just loved any excuse to get behind the wheel. I acquiesced politely, as any good guest would do.

Francine's was virtually empty. Francine herself was there but she wore a horrific scowl as she poured our coffee. Her demeanor was hardly befitting a proper proprietress, but I resisted the urge to point that out. Instead, I focused on the menu.

"What's got you looking so miserable this fine afternoon?" Gertie asked. "You been drinking that pickle juice again?"

"Stifle it, Gertie." Francine slammed the coffee pot onto our table. "I'm not in the mood."

Obviously not for niceties, that much was clear.

"What's wrong?" Aunt Ida Belle asked. "You need help with something?"

Francine sighed. "I'm sorry, it's been a long morning. Our refrigerator is acting up."

Fortune set her menu aside. "You want me to take a quick look at it?"

"No, but thanks for asking. It's under warranty, so that's not a problem." She shot a quick look over her shoulder. "The company sent a repairman out. He's the one giving me fits. Plain old rude, I'll tell you. He's in there grousing like it's an Olympic sport but not getting much done from what I can see."

I handed Francine my menu and scooted out of the booth. This was something I could handle. Honestly, I welcomed the distraction. "I'll just have a wee word with him," I said.

Francine's face was transformed by her grateful smile. "Thank you, hon. He's right through those double doors. I'll be with you as soon as I get the girls' order."

I slipped through the double doors, a mini-lecture ready to trip off my tongue, but the kitchen was empty. I looked around the small space. Where was Mr. Miserable? I inhaled and a drift of cigarette smoke wafted through the back door. I headed in that direction.

I pushed open the door. A man in denim overalls stood at the bottom of the steps with his back toward me. "Excuse me, sir. I'm going to ask you to put out that cigarette."

With a careless flick of his wrist, the man tossed his cigarette down onto the asphalt and turned around to face me. His expression certainly was surly, Francine wasn't wrong. Something in the way he looked stirred up a latent anger within me. I came down the last two steps toward him.

"Now, then, I'd like to have a word with you about your attitude when you're—"

But my next words were cut off about the time my oxygen supply was. Before I knew what he was about, he grabbed me around the waist with one hand and clamped his other hand over my mouth. Despite my thrashing about to free myself, he carried me like I was a rag doll toward a white van.

I struggled mightily when I saw the van door slide open and another man's hands reach for me. I wasn't sure what happened to women who were thrown in the back of a van, but I knew it was nothing good.

The second man's hands were rougher than the first. With far more force than was called for, he threw me against the opposite wall. The door slid closed behind him and I felt the van lurch forward. Panicked, my eyes swept through the back of the vehicle looking for another means of escape. There was another door, but a metal grate stood between me and an escape.

I did the only thing I could think of, I screamed. Like a banshee. Which turned out not to be the wisest move because the man reached over and backhanded me across the face. Hard. I touched my stinging face. "That was rude."

He hurled a few curse words in my direction. My head snapped up.

Russian. He'd spoken to me in Russian. I didn't know what the words meant, but I didn't need to. This wasn't a random kidnapping. This was a thousand times worse. These thugs were Sidorov henchmen. And I'd walked right into their trap.

Red hot hatred flowed through my veins like lava down a Hawaiian mountainside. I looked around wildly while I struggled to think what my options might be. My best guess was that we were traveling at least sixty miles per hour. Judging by the way the way the van was weaving back and forth, the driver was as erratic as Gertie.

Gertie. A ripple of hope ran through me. Fortune. Aunt Ida Belle. They'd find me gone and come after me. Which would put them in grave danger. My soaring spirits crashed and burned in one fell swoop. If it meant they were going to be in danger, I hoped they wouldn't find me.

I turned my attention back to the man who stood between me and freedom. His sneer was downright nasty. But what could he do besides smack me around a little? Somewhere, Vladimir was waiting for me to be brought to him. And I was quite sure he wanted me in one piece.

"Where are you taking me?" I demanded. "Where's Vladimir?"

Instead of answering me, he ignored me. Which really got under my skin. If I were writing a handbook on kidnapping etiquette, I certainly would have included polite conversation as a must-have.

As much to distract myself as to annoy him, I peppered him with questions for the duration of the drive. How much English he actually understood, I didn't care. If he didn't enjoy playing the role of a kidnapper, he could take that up with the Sidorovs.

The van came to a stop about fifteen minutes later. At least it felt like fifteen minutes, it could have been less. Or more. All I knew for certain was that I was hopping mad.

As soon as my feet were on the ground, I tried to pull away but idiot number two had a tight grip on me and I couldn't pull free. The bright afternoon sunshine hurt my eyes after being in the semi-dark van, but I looked around.

As best I could tell, our precise location was the middle of nowhere. Trees with dark green leaves provided a shaded canopy for a rather sad looking hunting cabin. Or maybe it was a fishing cabin. I could smell the bayou. I looked down at my feet and frowned. This mud was going to ruin my pumps.

A rough push from behind propelled me in the direction of the cabin. As I stumbled up onto the porch, the door swung open. One more good push got me through the doorway. I blinked as my eyes now had to adjust to the dark interior. I didn't know where we were, but I knew Vladimir Sidorov was here. I could smell him.

"Vladimir, didn't I mention to you more than once that you wear too much cologne?"

A low growl came from the opposite side of the room. By now I could see just enough to make out the form of my host for the afternoon's festivities. Equal parts disgust and anger swirled around inside of me. I felt curiously unafraid. Maybe because I knew that the odds of my making it out of here alive were so bad, even I wouldn't bet money on them.

I wished I'd let Aunt Ida Belle wire me before we'd gone to Francine's diner. Not that it would help much if no one knew where I was. Damn Vladimir.

I looked him up and down. He was overdressed and I told him so. "It seems you're intent on ignoring all of my lessons, aren't you? You wear a gray pinstripe three-piece suit to a meeting in the Louisiana bayou? Really? What about respecting the local culture? Denim jeans and a plaid shirt topped off by a baseball cap would have been far more appropriate."

Vladimir frowned. He turned to the van driver. "Did she hit her head?"

"Nyet," I snapped, using up just about all the Russian I knew. "I'm warning you that I'm not in a good mood." I stuck my right foot out so he could see the damage done to my shoe. "These are ruined thanks to your stupid choice of a rendezvous point."

From the way his face scrunched up at my use of the word "rendezvous", I knew Vladimir wasn't completely sure what it meant. But I wasn't about to dumb down my language for his sake.

I looked around. Shades were drawn over the windows, but I could see light streaming in through the back door's glass pane. What I didn't see were more of Vladimir's people. Was he really only here with the two who'd kidnapped me or were the others hiding? Not that it mattered. I wasn't about to make a run for it. I was trapped right in the middle of nowhere and I knew it.

"So, let's move this meeting right along," I said. "Why don't you confess to Misha's murder and we can be done with your little game?"

In lieu of an answer, Vladimir pulled a pistol out of his jacket pocket and pointed it straight at my head.

Chapter Fifteen

GUNSHOTS ERUPTED. ABOVE the sound of my own screams, I heard Vladimir scream, too. His wasn't a shout or a yell, but a full-on squeak-scream several octaves higher than I thought he'd be able to reach. As quickly as it began, the shooting stopped. Stunned, I opened my eyes.

Despite the volley of bullets, miraculously, no one had been hit. I barely had time to register the fact that I wasn't bleeding before I received my second shock. Fortune was standing behind Vladimir with a thin wire rope in her hands. She was securing his hands behind his back. And the reason he was letting her? Because my dear Aunt Ida Belle stood holding his gun in her hands, and it was leveled directly at his left temple.

"Hiya kid, you okay?"

I whirled around. Gertie held not one but two guns, and they were trained on the men who'd kidnapped me.

I struggled to get a lungful of oxygen. "What just happened?"

"Officially or unofficially?" Gertie grinned. "Because the answer depends on who's going to hear it."

"Unofficially?" I wasn't even sure, but I just wanted some sort of explanation. "How did you find me?"

Gertie pointed to Vladimir's henchmen with her weapons. "Loosey and Goosey here tore out of Sinful so fast that they aroused plenty of people's suspicion. Carter got a slew of calls at the police station just about the time we raced over there to report that you'd been kidnapped."

My knees threatened to buckle with relief. I couldn't believe they'd found me so quickly. And then the other shoe dropped. "Wait, you shot your way in here?" I didn't know if I should be horrified or impressed, but I knew I was grateful.

"We'll go over all that later," Aunt Ida Belle said, her voice thick with emotion. "For now, we're just happy you're okay." She cleared her throat. "Let's deal with these gorillas first."

I smiled. She really was an old dear. Gruff but loving. For the first time, I realized how lucky I was to have her as my aunt. I was lucky to have all three in my life, the life they'd just saved. My eyes filled with tears.

"Wow, hold on, it's not time for a meltdown yet," Fortune called. "We've got a confession to hear first. Don't we, Mr. Sidorov?" She tightened her hold on his arms and he swore.

Really, he just had to stop that.

"Why did you kill Misha?" I demanded. "What did he ever do to you?"

Vladimir spit in the direction of my shoes. I jumped back. My eyes narrowed.

"I'm just itching to plug one of these bullets into your useless head." Aunt Ida Belle jabbed his head with her gun. "Now, do you want to answer my niece's question or do you want to be shot?"

Vladimir growled.

Aunt Ida Belle cocked the trigger.

That action appeared to loosen Vladimir's tongue. "Mikhail was a spoiled brat. His whole life he was a major pain in the ass. But my father always saw him as the golden boy. The perfect little son. I was tired of the bullshit."

Again with the bull-sheet. "So you killed him?" I demanded.

Vladimir shrugged. "What do you care if I did? You didn't want him."

True enough, but hardly the point. I wanted a full confession, even if I wasn't wired.

"So what you're saying is that you're too much of a coward to admit the truth," I goaded him. "You killed Misha and yet you can't say it like a man." I hoped the "like a man" comment would be tantamount to waving a red cape in front of a bull.

"Yes, I killed Misha. He was a worthless bastard and I'm not sorry I poisoned him."

Olé!

The sound of sirens heralded the arrival of Sinful's finest. In yet another flurry of activity, Carter and his deputy burst into the cabin. I stood back against the wall and watched as Vladimir and his two lackeys were cuffed and taken out to the patrol car.

A moment later, Carter returned to stand in the doorway. He surveyed the scene, his eyes taking in the broken glass, shattered objects, and the disarray of the premises. He shook his head. "I won't even ask how you got here before I did or where you got those guns." He gave Aunt Ida Belle and Gertie a pointed look. "Just don't let me see them again."

Both women nodded.

Carter's eyes settled on Fortune. "Are you okay? You're not hurt?"

She smiled. "I'm fine. You go, we'll see you at the station. With a taped confession I know you'll want to hear."

I gasped. "But how? Who?"

Aunt Ida Belle lifted her shirt to expose a wire taped to a patch of the most wrinkled skin I'd ever seen. It was a beautiful sight. We had Vladimir's confession, and it wouldn't surprise me if he sang like a Russian songbird when interrogated.

Life in prison would be far preferable to what his father would do to him when he found out that it was Vladimir who'd killed Misha.

"Great," Carter looked pleased for the first time since I'd met him. "Get that down to the station right away, would you?"

"Absolutely," Aunt Ida Belle said. "There's just one thing we didn't get on tape. Vladimir told us that Misha's body is in a coffin at the bottom of the bayou right behind Fontenot's. That doesn't make any sense to me, but I thought you'd want to hear it."

I stared. Her innocent shrug was Oscar worthy. But as shocked as I was at her blatant lie, I was also pleased that Misha's body wouldn't be submerged for long.

Not even he deserved that.

SEVERAL HOURS AND ONE bubble bath later, I was once again ensconced in my pink satin robe. I settled into Gertie's sofa with a contented sigh. I had never been so grateful to be anywhere in my life. I looked at the three women who'd welcomed me to Sinful a couple of days earlier. They'd not only offered me a place to hide out, they'd saved my life today. How could I thank them properly?

"Well, that was fun." Gertie sat beside me, a bottle of cold beer in hand. "It was my first little go around with the Russian mob."

"Are you hungry, Stephanie?" Fortune gestured toward the kitchen. "Francine sent over several days' worth of meals. She feels terrible about what happened."

"I'm not hungry, but I am confused." I frowned. "How did Vladimir know we'd be at Francine's?"

"Well, now, that's my fault." Gertie's expression was apologetic. "I'd called the diner before lunch to ask Francine about today's special. I had a terrible hankering for chicken fried steak. I told her we'd be heading over in the afternoon. Best I can figure, our phone was bugged."

Ida Belle shook her head. "And there you were, acting like the idea to go to Francine's just popped into your head when you were fixin' to go all along."

"Trust me, I feel bad about it."

"Don't, please. You saved me." I felt my eyes mist up. I laid my hand over my heart. "I have to tell you all—"

Aunt Ida Belle scrambled to her feet, a look of horror on her face. "Don't cry, or give us a mushy speech." She looked at Fortune and Gertie, who wore equally horrified expressions. "We're not the overly emotional types." She smiled warmly. "We're happy that you're safe. That's all that matters."

I nodded. They might like to act tough as granite but they were softies at heart, all three. But I'd play along with their tough girl act if it was so important to them. "So, I guess it's time to look up bus schedules. I'll see if I can catch one tomorrow afternoon after I give Carter my statement."

"Let's not be hasty, Stephanie," Aunt Ida Belle said. "You've only been here a few days. There's no real reason to rush off, is there?"

I tried to keep a smile from my face, but I was unsuccessful. It felt good to know that I was wanted.

"Come to think of it," Gertie said, "you should spend the entire summer here with us. Once old man Sidorov gets wind of the fact that you got Vladimir to confess to killing Misha, he's going to be on the war path. You might be safer here than in Boston."

I hadn't thought of that. I had to admit that the idea of a long visit was appealing. "So you think Sinful's a decent place to hide out for awhile?"

Fortune laughed. "Oh, yeah, I'll vouch for that."

A Note from Caroline

Thank you so much for taking the time to read this book. I enjoyed writing it and hope that you enjoyed reading it enough to pick up the next in my Miss Prim and Proper Series, One Night in the Bayou.
Thanks to Jana DeLeon for her generosity in sharing her Miss Fortune world with other writers!
To learn more about my other books, please visit my website -
www.carolinemickelson.com[1]
I'd love to have you join my VIP Reader Newsletter so that you can be the first to hear about new releases, discounts, and contests. Join us!

---

1. http://www.carolinemickelson.com